NINE

The Musical

Book by
Arthur Kopit

Music and Lyrics by
Maury Yeston

Adaptation from the Italian by Mario Fratti
(*Based on Fellini's "8 1/2"*)

No part of this book may be reproduced, stored in a retrieval system, or transmitted in any form, by any means, including mechanical, electronic, photocopying, recording, or otherwise, without the prior written permission of the publisher.

SAMUEL FRENCH, INC.
45 WEST 25TH STREET   NEW YORK 10010
7623 SUNSET BOULEVARD   HOLLYWOOD 90046
LONDON   *TORONTO*

Book Copyright ©, 1983 by Arthur Kopit

LYRICS

"Amor" ©, 1982, 1984.
"Be Italian" ©, 1982, 1982.
"Be On Your Own" ©, 1982, 1982.
"The Bells of St. Sebastian" ©, 1982, 1984.
"A Call From The Vatican" ©, 1982, 1982.
"Every Girl in Venice" ©, 1982, 1984.
"Folies Bergeres" ©, 1982, 1982.
"Germans at the Spa" ©, 1982, 1984.
"Getting Tall" ©, 1982, 1982.
"The Grand Canal" ©, 1982, 1984.
"Guido's Song" ©, 1975, 1982.
"I Can't Make This Movie" ©, 1982, 1984.
"My Husband Makes Movies" ©, 1982, 1982.
"Nine" ©, 1975, 1982.
"Not Since Chaplin" ©, 1982, 1984.
"Only With You" ©, 1982, 1982.
"Only You" ©, 1982, 1984.
"Overture Delle Donne" ©, 1982, 1982.
"Simple" ©, 1982, 1982.
"Spa Music" ©, 1982, 1984.
"Ti Voglio Bene" ©, 1982, 1984.
"Unusual Way" ©, 1975, 1982.
"Waltz of Guido" ©, 1982, 1984.
"Contini Submits" ©, 1984.
"Marcia Dei Ragazzi" ©, 1984.

All of the above lyrics are © by Yeston Music Ltd.

Administered for the world by Dashon Music, Inc.
All rights reserved.

> Anyone presenting the play shall not commit or authorize any act or omission by which the copyright of the play or the right to copyright same may be impaired.
>
> No changes shall be made in the play for the purpose of your production unless authorized in writing.
>
> The publication of this play does not imply that it is necessarily available for performance by amateurs or professionals. Amateurs and professionals considering a production are strongly advised in their own interests to apply to Samuel French, Inc., for consent before starting rehearsals, advertising, or booking a theatre or hall.

Printed in U.S.A.

ISBN 0 573 68157 0

Amateurs wishing to arrange for the production of NINE must make application to SAMUEL FRENCH, INC., at 45 West 25th Street, New York, N. Y. 10010, giving the following particulars:

(1) The name of the town and theatre or hall in which it is proposed to give the production.
(2) The maximum seating capacity of the theatre or hall.
(3) Scale of ticket prices.
(4) The number of performances it is intended to give, and the dates thereof.
(5) The title, number of performances, gross receipts and amount of royalty and rental paid on your last musical performed.

Upon receipt of these particulars SAMUEL FRENCH, INC., will quote the amateur terms and availability.

Stock royalty and availability quoted on application to Samuel French, Inc.

For all other rights apply to Flora Roberts, Inc., 157 West 57th St., New York, N.Y. 10019.

An orchestration consisting of:

Conductor's Score
Piano/Vocal Score (Rehearsal Piano Score)
Reed I (Flute, Piccolo, Alto Flute, Recorder)
Reed II (Oboe, English Horn)
Reed III (Flute, Piccolo, Clarinet, Alto Saxophone)
Reed IV (Clarinet, Eb Clarinet, Bass Clarinet)
Reed V (Flute, Bassoon, Clarinet)
Horns I & II
Trumpets/Piccolo Trumpets I & II
Trombone I
Trombone II
Percussion I & II (Timpani, Xylophone, Chimes, Bells, Drums, etc.) (2 books)
Violins (6 players, 1 doubles on Mandolin) (3 books)
Violas I & II
Celli I & II
Bass
Harp
Keyboard (Harpsichord, Celeste, Electric Piano)
Chorus Books

will be loaned two months prior to the production ONLY on receipt of the royalty quoted for all performances, the rental fee and a refundable deposit. The deposit will be refunded on the safe return to SAMUEL FRENCH, INC. of all material loaned for the production.

IMPORTANT ADVERTISING AND BILLING REQUIREMENTS

The names of Arthur Kopit, Maury Yeston and Mario Fratti must receive billing in any and all advertising and publicity issued in connection with the licensing, leasing and renting of the show for stock and amateur production. This billing shall appear in, but not be limited to all theatre programs, houseboards, billboards, advertisements (except ABC ads), marquees, displays, posters, throwaways, circulars, announcements, and whenever and wherever the title of the show appears; and said billing must be on a separate line following the title of the show. In said billing the names of Arthur Kopit and Maury Yeston must be equal in size, type and prominence and at least Fifty Per Cent (50%) of the size of the title type, and the name of Mario Fratti must be in size of type no less than 75% the size of type of the names of Messrs. Kopit and Yeston. No credits may be larger than those credits afforded the Authors and Composers of the show except the title and the names of the stars appearing above the title. The billing must appear in the following form:

(Name of Producer)

presents

NINE

Book by
ARTHUR KOPIT

Music and Lyrics by
MAURY YESTON

Adaptation from the Italian by Mario Fratti
Broadway production directed by Tommy Tune
Original Cast Album on Columbia Records and Tapes

NINE opened at the 46th Street Theatre, New York City, on May 9, 1982. It was produced by Michel Stuart, Harvey J. Klaris, Roger S. Berlind, James M. Nederlander, Francine LeFrak and Kenneth D. Greenblatt. The musical was directed by Tommy Tune, the scenery was designed by Lawrence Miller, the costumes by William Ivey Long, and the lighting by Marcia Madeira. The cast was as follows:

GUIDO CONTINI	Raul Julia
GUIDO AT AN EARLY AGE	Cameron Johann
LUISA	Karen Akers
CARLA	Anita Morris
CLAUDIA	Shelly Burch
GUIDO'S MOTHER	Taina Elg
LILIANE LA FLEUR	Liliane Montevecchi
LINA DARLING	Laura Kenyon
STEPHANIE NECROPHORUS	Stephanie Cotsirilos
OUR LADY OF THE SPA	Kate Dezina
MAMA MADDELENA	Camille Saviola
SARRAGHINA	Kathi Moss
MARIA	Jeanie Bowers
A VENETIAN GONDOLIER	Colleen Dodson
GIULIETTA	Louise Edeiken
ANNABELLA	Nancy McCall
FRANCESCA	Kim Criswell
DIANA	Cynthia Meryl
RENATA	Rita Rehn
OLGA VON STURM	Dee Etta Rowe
HEIDI VON STURM	Linda Kerns
ILSA VON HESSE	Alaina Warren Zachary
GRETCHEN VON KRUPF	Lulu Downs
YOUNG GUIDO'S SCHOOLMATES	Jadrien Steele, Patrick Wilcox, Christopher Evans Allen

An initial staged reading of NINE was held at the Composer/Librettist Conference at the Eugene O'Neill Memorial Theatre Center.

CAST OF CHARACTERS

GUIDO CONTINI — the film director.
GUIDO AT AN EARLY AGE — (Little Guido).
LUISA CONTINI — Guido's wife.
CARLA ALBANESE — Guido's mistress.
CLAUDIA NARDI — the actress, Guido's former protegee.
GUIDO'S MOTHER
LILIANE LA FLEUR — Guido's producer. (MAURICE LA FLEUR if played by a man.)
LINA DARLING — La Fleur's mysterious accomplice. (LEO DARLING if played by a man.)
STEPHANIE NECROPHORUS — a critic. (STEFAN NECROPHORUS if played by a man.)
OUR LADY OF THE SPA
MAMA MADDELENA — chief of chambermaids.
SARRAGHINA — a voluptuous whore.

THE ITALIANS

DIANA
MARIA
FRANCESCA — (FRANCESCO if played by a man.)
ANNABELLA
GIULIETTA — (GIULIO if played by a man.)
RENATA — (RENATO if played by a man.)
A VENETIAN GONDOLIER — (may be played by a man or woman.)

THE GERMANS

OLGA VON STURM — (OTTO VON STURM if played by a man.)
HEIDI VON STURM
ILSA VON HESSE
GRETCHEN VON KRUPF (HANS VON KRUPF if played by a man.)
LITTLE GUIDO'S THREE SCHOOLMATES — (Boys.)
A NUN — (NOTE: This character appears *only* in the cross-overs on pp. 15 and 40 and in the scolding scene on p. 47. She should not be confused with SARRAGHINA, who is dressed as a nun from her first entrance on p. 43 until she discards her habit on p. 44, and who reappears in the nun costume on p. 47.)

MUSICAL NUMBERS

ACT I

OVERTURE	Company	15
SPA MUSIC		
NOT SINCE CHAPLIN		
GUIDO'S SONG	Guido	19
CODA DI GUIDO	Company	21
THE GERMANS AT THE SPA	Mama Maddelena, Italians, Germans	22
MY HUSBAND MAKES MOVIES	Luisa	27
A CALL FROM THE VATICAN	Carla	28
ONLY WITH YOU	Guido	31
FOLIES BERGERES	La Fleur, Necrophorus and Company	35
NINE	Guido's Mother and Company	41
TI VOGLIO BENE/BE ITALIAN	Sarraghina, Boys and Company	45
THE BELLS OF ST. SEBASTIAN	Guido, Boys and Company	47

ACT TWO

A MAN LIKE YOU/UNUSUAL WAY/DUET	Claudia and Guido	52
THE GRAND CANAL	Guido and Company	53
CONTINI SUBMITS/THE GRAND CANAL/ TARANTELLA/		
EVERY GIRL IN VENICE/MARCIA DI RAGAZZI/ RECITATIVO/		
AMOR/RECITATIVO/ONLY YOU/FINALE		
SIMPLE	Carla	62
BE ON YOUR OWN	Luisa	63
I CAN'T MAKE THIS MOVIE	Guido	64
GETTING TALL	Little Guido	66
REPRISE: LONG AGO/NINE	Guido	67

MUSICAL NUMBERS — COMPLETE LIST

1	Overture
2	After Overture
3	Spa Music
4	Not Since Chaplin
5	Guido's Song
6	The Germans at the Spa
6A	La Fleur's Entrance
6B	Garden Scene
6C	Reporter's Return
6D	My Husband Makes Movies
6E	After Movies
7	A Call from the Vatican
7A	Western di Guido
7B	The Bible
7C	Documentary
8	Only With You
8A	After Only with You
8B	Claudia
8C	The Critic
9	The Script
10	Folies Bergeres
10A	After Folies
10B	Gong di Guido
11	Nine
12	Samba di Guido #1
13	Samba di Guido #2
13A	Chant di Guido
14A	Be Italian part 1
14B	Be Italian part 2
14C	Be Italian part 3
14D	Be Italian part 4
14E	After Be Italian
15	The Bells of St. Sebastian
16	Entr'acte
16B	Beach Scene
17	A Man Like You
17A	Unusual Way
18A	Contini Submits/Grand Canal
18B	Tarantella I
18E	Every Girl in Venice
18F	Marcia di Ragazzi
18G	Curtain Music

NINE

- 18H Recitative & Aria: Amor
- 18I Guido Nervoso I
- 18J Critic and Mama
- 18L Guido Nervoso II
- 18M Recitative & Cavatina: Only You
- 18N B Minor Tarantella
- 18O Tarantella II
- 18P Grand Canal Finale
- 18Q After Grand Canal
- 19   Simple
- 20   Be On Your Own
- 21   Luisa's Exit
- 22   I Can't Make This Movie
- 23   Waltz from Nine
- 24   Getting Tall
- 25   Reprises
- 26   Bows
- 27   Exit Music

The alternate Grand Canal Sequence is labeled as follows:
- 18A Grand Canal Sequence part 1
- 18B Grand Canal Sequence part 2

Parts are also available for the following numbers in alternate keys:
- 6D My Husband Makes Movies (coupled with 6C Reporters' Return) up a tone to B flat major — piano and conductor scores available.
- 7   A Call from the Vatican — down a tone to B flat major
- 11 Nine — down a major third to A flat major — conductor score available
- 15 The Bells of St. Sebastian — down a tone to G minor
- 20 Be On Your Own — up a tone to E minor — piano score available.

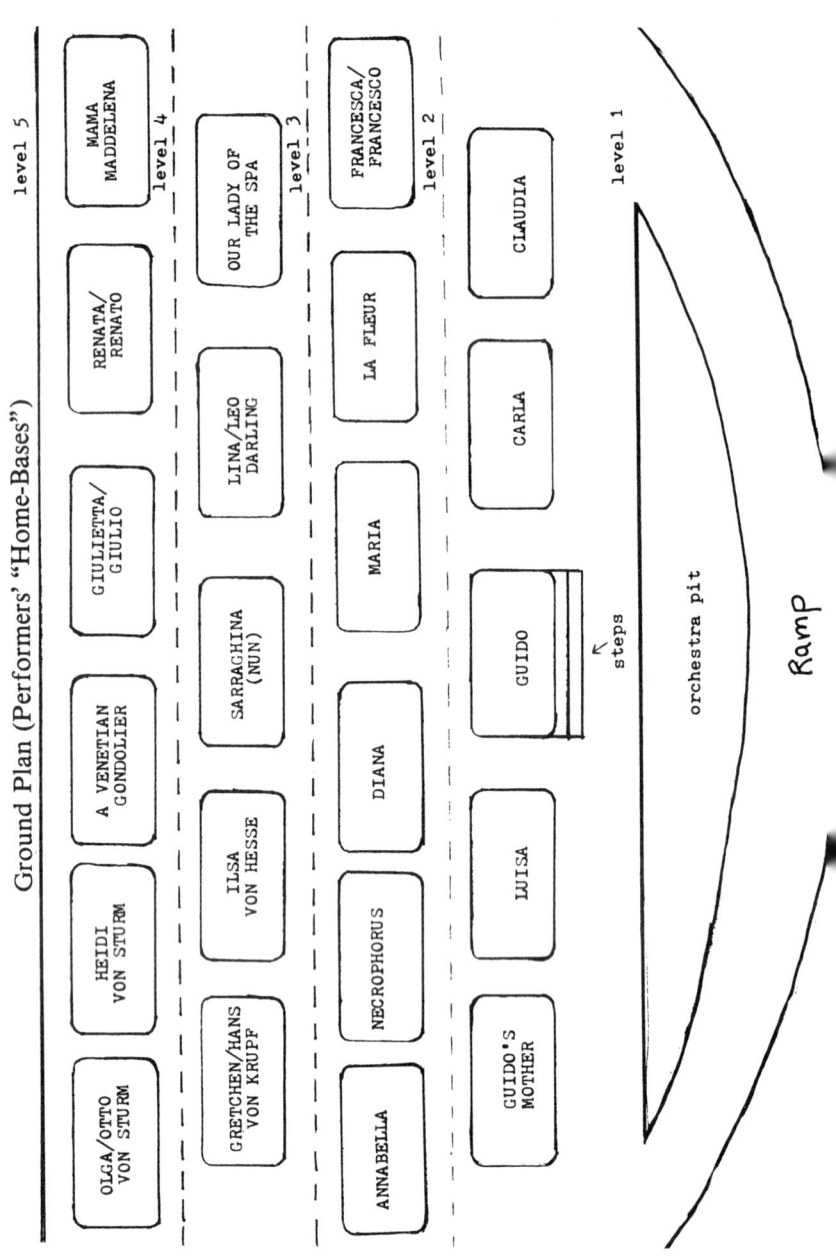

Nine

ACT ONE

As the house-lights dim, a church bell rings nine times.

Lights up on a large white-tiled room; enormous windows in the rear. Around the room there are white-tiled boxes. The place bears a resemblance to a steambath in a sanitorium or a spa. The sense is conveyed of a dreamspace — perhaps one by Magritte or De Chirico. Sitting on a box DS. is GUIDO CONTINI, the renowned film director. Nearby is his wife LUISA. LUISA is talking to GUIDO, but GUIDO's mind is elsewhere.

LUISA. Guido, mi stai ascoltando? He was a teacher of mine from school, a priest. I hadn't seen him in *years.* Anyway, he was amazed to hear I was married to you. He said, "What's it like being married to Guido Contini?"

(*A woman's sensuous laugh is heard from offstage. LUISA continues to talk, but in Italian and softer, telling GUIDO that she'd like to spend more time alone with him, describing the dinner she's prepared for him, recalling the events of her day. The focus of our attention shifts to the woman about to enter GUIDO's thoughts: CARLA.*)

CARLA. (*entering saucily, unnoticed by LUISA*) Oh, Guido, Guido, Guido! Just to think of him my heart comincia fare boompa-boompa — you should feel it. Guido e mio amore. It's true. And what's more, I know Guido e completamente innamorato di me! You see, I know what Guido really needs. *I* am what Guido really needs. If only my husband would give me a divorce — then Guido could get *his* divorce, and we could get married! (*CARLA and LUISA continue to speak as GUIDO'S MOTHER enters. CARLA wonders how LUISA can live with a man who doesn't love her, then details her bland life with her husband.*)

GUIDO'S MOTHER. I have never understood any of my son's films. It's true. I never know what Guido is thinking. I never knew — even when he was a child.

NECROPHORUS. (*entering*) Guido Contini is a charlatan! To see a film directed by Contini is to experience a world — no, not a world, a *conceit* out of touch with reality. It's no wonder to me that his last three films have been flops. Oh, I know most of you think Guido Contini is a genius. A cantaloupe is a genius compared to Contini! (*From offstage, a clap of hands is heard.*) Ah, forgive me. I am not used to being a film producer. I am used to being a critic. (*NECROPHORUS beckons and LA FLEUR enters with a flourish.*)

LA FLEUR. Bon soir! I have not always been an intellectual!

(*NOTE: From this point until GUIDO's interruption, entrances and speeches overlap, slowly building to a cacophonous crescendo.*)

(*DIANA and MARIA enter together, as NECROPHORUS continues to critique CONTINI's films in English and Greek:* "They lack coherence, they lack cohesiveness. What kind of a world is Contini dealing with?" *LA FLEUR meanwhile recalls in French, memories of the Folies Bergeres.*)

DIANA. (*upon entering, with a British accent*) Guido told you what?

(*LINA/LEO DARLING enters, as DIANA and MARIA continue the dialogue below:*)

LINA/LEO DARLING. Guido! (*LINA/LEO whispers in LA FLEUR's ear.*)
LA FLEUR. Quoi? (*To the audience:*) Excusez-moi. Cette personne vient toujours m'embeter. (*To LINA/LEO:*) C'est pas vrai!
LINA/LEO. Guido!
LA FLEUR. Guido!
FRANCESCA/FRANCESCO. (*entering, to LA FLEUR*) Ma cherie (Mon cher)!

(*FRANCESCA/FRANCESCO continues talking as MAMA MADDELENA, ANNABELLA, GIULIETTA/GIULIO, and RENATA/RENATO enter together, speaking the dialogue below. We are now seeing GUIDO's two prime realities: his wife and his imagination. As always, LUISA never notices any of these other women because they are in GUIDO's mind.*)

NINE

It's Guido that I really want to meet. Guido Contini makes the most wonderful films. I've seen every film that Guido ever made. (*FRANCESCA/FRANCESCO and LA FLEUR chat.*)

MARIA. (*continued from above*) Guido ha detto che la part' e mia.
DIANA. Guido?
MARIA. Guido!
DIANA. But Guido gave the part to me.
MARIA. No, Guido ha dato la parte a me.
DIANA. To you?
MARIA. A me!
DIANA. Guido?
MARIA. Guido se stesso!
DIANA. Well, I'm going to ask Guido.
MARIA. Perche? Non e necessario.
DIANA. Because Guido gave the part to me.
MARIA. Ma non hai la parte, signorina!
DIANA. I do so have the part—Guido promised.
MARIA. Quale promessa? Va chiedere a Guido!
DIANA. Where is Guido?
MARIA. Guido e a casa mia.
DIANA. Guido's at your house?
MARIA. E nel mio letto.
DIANA. Guido's in your bed? (*MARIA nods.*) I thought he was in my bed.
MARIA. Basta, la part' e schifosa.
DIANA. He showed you the script?
MARIA. Si, naturalmente.
DIANA. What a shit! (*DIANA and MARIA look at one another and laugh. They chat.*)
MAMA MADDELENA. (*as she enters*) Guido Contini is a prince. He's a crazy man, but he's a prince. And he's a prince who loves everybody. At this moment, he's loving someone on the first floor, (*Four GERMANS enter—OLGA/OTTO VON STURM, HEIDI VON STURM, ILSA VON HESSE, and GRETCHEN/HANS VON KRUPF.*) on the second floor, on the third floor, on the fourth floor, in the dining room, in the lobby, in the basement, on the roof, on the terrace, in the gardens, on the staircase, in the sauna. Such energy. Che uomo!
GIULIETTA/GIULIO & RENATA/RENATO. (*as they enter*) Guido!
RENATA/RENATO. (*peering through a keyhole*) Il Signor Contini e qui ai bagni! (*RENATA/RENATO calls GIULIETTA/*

GIULIO, *who has been staring into space, to come look through the keyhole.*)

GIULIETTA/GIULIO. (*looking*) What's that?

ANNABELLA. (*as she enters*) Guido. Perche? Perche, signor? Perche me ne rimuneri cosi? Questa e la mia vita! Guido! . . . In my dream, Guido sees me and smiles. He comes over, we're in a crowd. He takes off my dress, no one seems to notice. I lie down on a coffee table, and he has me there on the table. When it's over, he says, "Yes, I think you'll be wonderful in my new film" — and I become a star. Could it happen? Perhaps. One must never give up hope.

GERMANS. (*as they enter*) Ein, ein, ein zwei drei. Ein, ein, ein zwei drei. Ein, ein, ein zwei drei. Guido!

(*CLAUDIA, OUR LADY OF THE SPA, and A VENETIAN GONDOLIER enter as the GERMANS continue simultaneously.*)

OLGA. Guido hast ein mund das treiben zum loo-loo. Guido ist mein wundermensch. Gott, wenn Guido's mund auf mein brust, meine beine, mein popo, mein kleine fusse. Heilige musik! Guido ist der mann auf meinem traumen.

OTTO. Guido's filmen sind ausgezeichnet — mit vielen schonen Damen. Ach, die brusten, die beinen, die kleinen fussen das treiben zum loo-loo. Heilige musik! Guido ist ein fuhrender Geist!

HEIDI. Guido hast augen das treiben zum foo-foo. Gott, wenn nur sein augen war auf meine nakte und Germanisch leib. Gott, wenn Guido spielen auf meine beine, meine grosse popo. Himmel! Guido ist der mann auf meinem traumen.

ILSA. Guido hast hande das treiben zum coo-coo! Gott, wenn nur zein hande paddling mein popo. In Hamburg, das existet nicht. Ach, Guido ahn meine beine spielt, ahn meine brust. Guido ist der mann auf meinem traumen. Ich liebe Guido!

GRETCHEN. Guido hast ein popo das treiben zum ga-ga! Guido ist mein wundermensch! Guido spielen auf meine grosse brust, meine grosse tum-tum! Ah, toten reich! Zu helfen mir!

HANS. Guido's filmen sind ausgezeichnet — mit vielen schonen Damen. Gott, die grossen brusten, die grossen tum-tum das treiben zum ga-ga! Toten reich! Zu helfen mir!

OLGA/OTTO. (*continued*) Ah, (Fraulein,) komm! Ein, ein, ein zwei drei! (*The GERMANS join in as CLAUDIA begins to sing*

NINE

GUIDO's name, and as DIANA and MARIA continue with the following:)

MARIA. Baciatemi. (*MARIA and DIANA kiss.*)

DIANA. Wait a minute, if Guido showed you the script, that means you got the part.

MARIA. Si, e vero! (*MARIA pushes DIANA.*)

DIANA. Come back here, you tart!

(*They fight. LA FLEUR breaks it up. A NUN enters. All the (men and) women start calling and singing the name of GUDIO.*

GUIDO, sensing his control in jeopardy, rises like a conductor and takes to his box as if it were a podium. Indeed, he even raises a baton and brings the (men and) women to silence and attention. They sit on their respective boxes. GUIDO, baton in hand, begins to conduct them in an OVERTURE.)

GUIDO. One, two, three, four . . .

(*The OVERTURE is sung.*)

LUISA. (*as the OVERTURE comes to an end*) Guido, I have to tell you, this is just not my idea of a successful marriage. (*GUIDO conducts a chord.*)

GUIDO. What? (*chord*)

LUISA. You told me we were going to spend the evening *talking!* I don't think you've heard a word I've said all night! (*chord*)

GUIDO. Luisa, that's not true. I've heard everything you've said. Everything. (*chord*)

LUISA. What I miss most, I think, is honesty. (*chord*)

GUIDO. Luisa, darling, believe me, I think you are the most honest woman I have ever met. (*chord*)

LUISA. (*coldly*) Thank you. Guido, how would you like a divorce? (*chord*)

GUIDO. (*his mind on his "orchestra"*) What? (*chord*)

LUISA. Because if you don't change your ways, I am going to *leave* you! (*That gets through. Huge chord.*)

GUIDO. (*quieting the chord*) Luisa, darling, listen, this is not a good moment in my life.

LUISA. Nor in mine! (*chord*)

GUIDO. As it happens, at this moment I have a great many things on my mind.

LUISA. (*like ice*) I can imagine. (*chord*)

CARLA. (*rising saucily and singing*) AHHHHHHH...!
GUIDO. (*panicking*) Down! Get down!
LUISA. (*as CARLA gets down*) Guido, are you paying attention to me?
GUIDO. Absolutely!
LA FLEUR. Contini! Are you trying to avoid me?
GUIDO. Absolutely not!
LA FLEUR. I certainly hope not. (*LA FLEUR's mysterious accomplice, LINA/LEO, points a small gun at GUIDO, who raises his arms in panic.*)
GUIDO'S MOTHER. (*sings*) GUIDO!
GUIDO. Mama! (*LITTLE GUIDO enters on a run.*)
GUIDO'S MOTHER. (*looking at LITTLE GUIDO*) Guido, where are you running to? Guido... (*LITTLE GUIDO runs over to her and hugs her. GUIDO hugs himself, his eyes shut, smiling at the memory.*)
GUIDO. Mama, Mama, Mama—
LUISA. (*with alarm*) Guido, are you all right?
GUIDO. Of course I'm all right! Why do you always ask me that? I am not a child! (*NECROPHORUS laughs mockingly.*) I am a mature Italian film director! (*Others pick up the laugh.*) And as such, perfectly capable of conducting my own affairs! (*silencing them*) Ssssh! (*turning to LUISA*) Luisa, listen, I've got an idea. Why don't we go away together? You know, someplace quiet, where I can clear my mind. And live like a monk.

(*MUSIC. Venice begins to appear on the horizon. OUR LADY OF THE SPA comes forward with an enticing, soothing smile.*)

OUR LADY OF THE SPA. Here in Venice, at Fontane di Luna, Europe's most exclusive spa, rejuvenation awaits you.
GUIDO. A spa! That's where we'll go! *Fontane di Luna!*
OUR LADY OF THE SPA. At Fontane di Luna there are waters fed by springs coming from somewhere deep, deep down—springs of purity and health, springs renowned for their amazing restorative powers.
GUIDO. It's what I *need!*
OUR LADY OF THE SPA. With these mysterious waters we caress and soothe—
GUIDO. (*to LUISA, trying to charm her*) I can lie in a tub! Up to here! And only *you* will know who I am.

NINE

Our Lady of the Spa. Emerging from your tub, you will find us waiting to embrace you with soft, warm linen towels. (*GUIDO begs LUISA with his eyes.*)
    Luisa. All right. But it's the last chance I'm giving you.
    Guido. It's all I ask! All I need!

(*MUSIC. Venice becomes clearer. We are at the spa.*)

    Our Lady of the Spa. The spa was built in 1443 by Michelozzo as the summer residence of the notorious Pope Innocenti III, better known to history as Il Bastardo. The miraculous mineral fountain around which the palazzo was constructed is over here in the garden.
    Luisa. It looks a bit like a convent school I once went to.
    Guido. It looks like my old parochial school. (*GUIDO starts to hide his face with his scarf.*)
    Luisa. Guido, what are you doing?
    Guido. Making sure no one recognizes me. A lot of famous people come to this place, you know.
    Luisa. Guido —
    Guido. What?
    Luisa. If you don't want to be recognized, why don't we go to a spa that's less well-known?
    Guido. Because if I do *that,* people will get the idea that I'm *hiding!*
    American Reporter. Guarda! It's Guido Contini!
    Guido. Oh my God!
    Guido & Luisa. (*together*) Reporters! (*LITTLE GUIDO runs off.*)
    Giulietta/Giulio. Guido Contini!
    Renata/Renato. Guido Contini!
    Reporters & Spa People. Guido Contini is here at the spa! (*sing*)
NOT SINCE CHARLIE CHAPLIN HAS THERE EVER BEEN
A FILM DIRECTOR LIKE THIS — GUIDO CONTINI!
    Guido. This is not what I wanted.
    Reporters & Spa People.
EVERYTHING HE DOES GETS WORLD ATTENTION
WHETHER IT'S A HIT OR A MISS — GUIDO CONTINI!
    Guido. (*to LUISA*) There's something I forgot to tell you.
    British Reporter. What're you doing here, Guido?
    American Reporter. Is it true your next project is in trouble?
    German Reporter. We understand your producer's suing you for breach of contract!

GUIDO. Please! One at a time! No one's suing me! And what makes anyone think my next project is in trouble?
REPORTERS & SPA PEOPLE. (*sing*)
HE WRITES THE SCRIPT!
GUIDO. It's going to be wonderful!
REPORTERS & SPA PEOPLE.
HE WRITES THE SCORE!
GUIDO. Make a lot of money!
REPORTERS & SPA PEOPLE.
HE'S THE DIRECTOR!
GUIDO. Win a lot of prizes!
REPORTERS & SPA PEOPLE.
AND EVEN MORE
HE'S A CONSUMMATE ACTOR!
GUIDO. Thank you, that's very kind of you.
LUISA. (*icily*) *What* next project?
GUIDO. I was going to tell you this evening.
AMERICAN REPORTER. So what's your new film about, Guido?
GUIDO. I do not discuss a script until I've finished writing it!
GERMAN REPORTER. Your producer claims you haven't even started it.
GUIDO. That's ridiculous! Where is she/he?
GERMAN REPORTER. In Paris.
AMERICAN REPORTER. Trying to find you.
BRITISH REPORTER. Does your wife know you're traveling with this woman? (*gestures toward LUISA*)
GUIDO. This *is* my wife.
CARLA. (*sings*)
GUIDO . . . !
GUIDO. Carla! My God! What're you doing here in Venice? (*He sneaks away from LUISA and pulls CARLA aside.*)
CARLA. I had to see you right away. I'm staying at the Albergo Caldo, numero cinque-cinque—
GUIDO. Cinque-cinque.
CARLA. I have wonderful news to tell you. I'll be waiting! (*They return to their former positions.*)
LUISA. Guido, was that Carla?
GUIDO. Carla? No-no my love—that's all over with.
CLAUDIA. (*appearing as if in a dream, sings*)
GUIDO . . . !
GUIDO. *Claudia!* I've been trying to reach you! I need you for my film!

NINE

OUR LADY OF THE SPA. Signor Contini, telephone, line seven; it's from Paris!

GUIDO. Claudia?

LA FLEUR. No, it's Liliane/Maurice La Fleur, your producer. Remember me?

GUIDO. (*gloomily*) Oh yes.

LA FLEUR. I still haven't seen a script! What are you doing in Venice?

GUIDO. Well, I'm, I'm . . . (*thinking fast*) scouting locations!

LA FLEUR. I see! That must mean the film's going to be *shot* in Venice. Thanks for telling me. I'll see you tomorrow.

GUIDO. (*even more gloomily*) Wonderful.

REPORTERS & SPA PEOPLE. (*sing*)
NO TASK TOO BIG!

GUIDO. So she's coming *here!*

REPORTERS & SPA PEOPLE.
NO TASK TOO SMALL!

GUIDO. Now what do I do?

REPORTERS & SPA PEOPLE.
HE SKETCHES COSTUMES!

GUIDO. (*brightly*) I'll go to Paris!

REPORTERS & SPA PEOPLE.
AND THAT'S NOT ALL
HE WRITES THE SUBTITLES!

(*GUIDO rejects the Paris idea.*)

OUR LADY OF THE SPA. Signor Contini, telephone, line five, it's the Hollywood Reporter!

GUIDO. Luisa, please help me! (*to REPORTERS*) If you don't mind, no more questions. I'll hold a press conference tomorrow. (*All return to their boxes.*)

GUIDO. (*sings*)
I WOULD LIKE TO BE HERE.
I WOULD LIKE TO BE THERE.
I WOULD LIKE TO BE EVERYWHERE AT ONCE—
I KNOW THAT'S A CONTRADICTION IN TERMS.
AND IT'S A PROBLEM, ESPECIALLY WHEN
MY BODY'S CLEARING FORTY AS MY MIND IS NEARING TEN.

I CAN HARDLY STAY UP,
AND I CAN'T GET TO SLEEP,
AND I DON'T WANT TO WAKE TOMORROW MORNING

AT THE BOTTOM OF SOME HEAP.
BUT WHY TAKE IT SO SERIOUSLY?
AFTER ALL, THERE'S NOTHING AT STAKE HERE —
  ONLY ME.

I WANT TO BE YOUNG,
AND I WANT TO BE OLD.
I WOULD LIKE TO BE WISE BEFORE MY TIME
AND YET BE FOOLISH AND BRASH AND BOLD.
I WOULD LIKE THE UNIVERSE TO GET DOWN ON ITS
  KNEES
AND SAY, "GUIDO, WHATEVER YOU PLEASE,
IT'S OKAY EVEN IF IT'S IMPOSSIBLE,
WE'LL ARRANGE IT."
THAT'S ALL THAT I WANT.

I AM LUSTING FOR MORE,
SHOULD I SETTLE FOR LESS?
I ASK YOU, WHAT'S A GOOD THING FOR
IF NOT FOR TAKING IT TO EXCESS?
ONE LIMITATION I DEARLY REGRET:
THERE'S ONLY ONE OF ME I'VE EVER MET.

I WOULD LIKE TO HAVE ANOTHER ME TO TRAVEL
  ALONG WITH MYSELF.
I WOULD EVEN LIKE TO BE ABLE TO SING A DUET
  WITH MYSELF.

I WOULD LIKE TO BE HERE
  (SING ALONG WITH MYSELF IN A SONG)
TO BE THERE
  (WALKING DOWN A LANE NOW, EVERYWHERE)
EVERYWHERE
  (EVERYWHERE, THAT'S A CONTRADICTION IN TERMS)
I WANT TO BE HERE
  (WITH A COUNTER—)
HERE (MELODY IN THE)
HERE (TOP OF THE MORNING TO YOU, GUIDO)
GUIDO (GUIDO)
GUIDO (GUIDO)
GUIDO. (ME)
ME (ME)
I WANT TO BE PROUST

NINE

OR THE MARQUIS DE SADE.
I WOULD LIKE TO BE CHRIST, MOHAMMED, BUDDHA
BUT NOT HAVE TO BELIEVE IN GOD,
AND YOU KNOW I MEAN IT WITH ALL OF MY HEART—
IT'S THE END IF SOMETHING IMPORTANT DOESN'T
  START . . .

I WANT TO BE YOUNG,
BUT I HAVE TO BE OLD.
WHAT I WANT IS A TALE OF SOUND AND FURY
THAT SOME IDIOT WENT AND TOLD.
I WOULD LIKE THE UNIVERSE TO GET DOWN ON ITS
  KNEES
AND SAY, "GUIDO, WHATEVER YOU PLEASE,
IT'S OKAY EVEN IF IT'S RIDICULOUS,
WE'LL ARRANGE IT . . ."

SO ARRANGE IT!
  ALL.
ARRANGE IT!
  GUIDO.
THAT'S ALL THAT I WANT!

(*ALL sing a musical flourish of praise to GUIDO: CODA DI GUIDO. LITTLE GUIDO enters to conduct with GUIDO.*)

  ALL.
CONTINI, CONTINI, CONTINI, CONTINI
CONTINI, CONTINI, CONTINI, CONTINI
GUIDO
  GUIDO. See what I mean?
  ALL.
GUIDO!

Scene: ANOTHER PART OF THE SPA

MAMA MADDELENA. Chambermaids! (Busboys!) Everybody! Tutti pronti! Come on! Diana!
DIANA. (*dressing and posing for GUIDO*) Here oye am!
MAMA MADDELENA. Snap to! Button up! What're you, auditioning for the maestro? Where's Renata/Renato?
RENATA/RENATO. (*peering through a keyhole*) Sono qui!

MAMA MADDELENA. What you doing there? Get away from there! Go get the sheets and blankets in the North Wing and bring them to the South Wing! And Maria!

MARIA. (*waking*) Ecco mi!

MAMA MADDELENA. Wake up! Come on! Get the pillowcases in the South Wing and bring them to the North Wing! And Giulietta/Giulio! Giulietta/Giulio! GIULIETTA/GIULIO!

GIULIETTA/GIULIO. Here, Mama!

MAMA MADDELENA. She/he *thinks* she's/he's here! God save us! Giulietta/Giulio, go get the towels from the steambath and bring them to the mud bath and don't drop them in the mud! And hurry up! (*FRANCESCA/FRANCESCO rises and joins the others.*) They'll be here any second! (*to GUIDO, who is following the action as if considering its cinematic possibilities*) Maestro . . . sono pronta. (*She sings.*)

	CHAMBERMAIDS (& BUSBOYS). (*sing*)
CLEAR THE DECKS, BE ALERT.	WE'LL CLEAR THE DECKS, WE'LL BE ALERT.
FIX YOUR TIE, FIX YOUR SKIRT.	WE'LL FIX OUR TIE AND SKIRT,
BE PREPARED TO CHANGE A FOREIGN COIN.	BE PREPARED TO CHANGE A FOREIGN COIN: DEUTSCHMARKS, FRANCS, KRONER, PFENNIGS, SHILLINGS.
YOU ALL KNOW WHAT TO DO.	WE ALL KNOW WHAT TO DO.
THEY'RE ON THEIR WAY, YOU KNOW WHO.	THEY'RE ON THEIR WAY, WE KNOW WHO.
EINS, ZWEI, DREI, VIER, FUNF, SECHS, SIEBEN, ACHT, NEUN.	DREI, VIER, FUNF, SECHS, SIEBEN, ACHT, NEUN.

MAMA MADDELENA.
THE GERMANS AT THE SPA,
THE GERMANS AT THE SPA,
THEY'LL SOON BE ARRIVING HERE TO SPEND

NINE

A LOST WEEK-END IN SHANGRI-LA.
THE GERMANS AT THE SPA
DESCEND FROM GERMAN MOUNTS.
THEY'VE COME TO TAKE THE WATERS
WITH THE DAUGHTERS OF ITALIAN COUNTS.

   Mama Maddelena, Chambermaids (& Busboys).
HOW WE LOVE TO HAVE THE GERMANS AT THE SPA—
CAREFULLY AVOIDING ANY SLIGHT FAUX-PAS.
FOR THE GERMANS AT THE SPA,
FOR THE GERMANS AT THE SPA,
FOR THE GERMANS ALLES MUST BE PERFECT.

THE GERMANS ARE COMING,
THE GERMANS ARE COMING,
ROLL OUT THE WIENERSCHNITZ,
ROLL OUT THE WIENERSCHNITZ.
THEY'LL SOON BE ARRIVING,
THE SPA WILL BE THRIVING.
THEY'LL COME, THEY'LL SIT, THEY'LL SCHVITZ.
THEY'LL COME, THEY'LL SIT, THEY'LL SCHVITZ.

BE SURE THERE'S LOTS OF GERMAN MUSIC
PLAYING.

UND WAS DU TUST IN MEINEM BRUST.
O MEIN GELIEBTER, O MEINE HERZ,
   ALLE GELIEBTER, UND SO WEITER.

Mama Maddelena.	Italians. (*one at a time*)
GO MOW THE LAWNS.	I'LL MOW THE LAWNS.
GO COOL THE BEER.	I'LL COOL THE BEER.
GO SHELL THE PRAWNS.	I'LL SHELL THE PRAWNS.
I THINK THEY'RE HERE.	THEY'RE HERE.

   Germans.
VE'RE HERE, VE'RE HERE,
THE GERMANS AT THE SHPA,
THE GERMANS AT THE SHPA.
VE JUST GOT IN A MINUTE AGO

'CAUSE GERMANY IS FILLED VIT SNOW.
TOGETHER NOW HOORAH
FOR THE GERMANS AT THE SHPA.
   MAMA MADDELENA.
OF ANYTHING THEY COULD HAVE CHOSEN,
WHY DO THEY WEAR LEDERHOSEN?
   GERMANS.
HOW VE LOVE TO SPIELEN AT OUR FAV'RITE SHPA,
CAREFULLY AVOIDING ALL THE FRENCH BOURGEOIS.
FOR THE GERMANS AT THE SHPA,
FOR THE GERMANS AT THE SHPA,
FOR THE GERMANS ALLES MUST BE GERMAN.

THE GERMANS ARE LAUGHINK,
VE'RE ALL PHOTOGRAPHINK,
VE CLICK THE HASSELBLAD,
VE CLICK THE HASSELBLAD.
UND JETZT VE'RE UNPACKINK.
IF NOTHING IS LACKINK,
VE TAKE A PROMENADE,
VE TAKE A PROMENADE.

AND VOT'S THAT LOVELY MUSIC I HEAR
PLAYING?

UND WAS DU TUST IN MEINEM BRUST.
O MEIN GELIEBTER, O MEINE HERZ,
  ALLE GELIEBTER, UND SO WEITER.
   HEIDI.
JUST VUNCE A YEAR I CAN ROMANCE BENEATH THE
  DANCE OF AN ITALIAN APRICOT MOON.
   GRETCHEN/HANS.
UND VUNCE A YEAR I CAN BE MORE THAN JUST
  ANOTHER TYCOON.
   GERMANS.
TOO SOON THIS ALL SHALL PASS.
   MAMA MADDELENA & ITALIANS.
THE GERMANS AT THE SPA
ARE EATING HALEVAH
AND CLOSING A DEAL FOR OIL
WITH A NOTED MIDDLE EASTERN SHAH.
   GERMANS.
VE EXERCISE BY DAY,

NINE

AT NIGHT WE SING UND PLAY.
I'M DANCING VIT ISOLDE—
VEN I HOLD 'ER EVERYTHING'S O.K.
    Mama Maddelena & Italians.
HOW WE LOVE TO SEE THE GERMANS AT THE SPA.
    Germans.
HOW VE LOVE TO BE THE GERMANS AT THE SHPA.
    All.
FOR THE GERMANS AT THE S(H)PA,
FOR THE GERMANS AT THE S(H)PA,
FOR THE GERMANS ITALY IS HEAVEN.

    Italians.
THE GERMANS ARE
  COMING,
THE GERMANS ARE
  COMING,
ROLL OUT THE WIENER-
  SCHNITZ,
ROLL OUT THE WIENER-
  SCHNITZ.
THEY'LL SOON BE
  ARRIVING,
THE SPA WILL BE
  THRIVING.
THEY'LL COME, THEY'LL
  SIT, THEY'LL SCHVITZ.
THEY'LL COME, THEY'LL
  SIT, THEY'LL SCHVITZ.
BE SURE THERE'S LOTS
  OF GERMAN MUSIC
  PLAYING!

HOW WE LOVE TO HAVE
THE GERMANS AT THE—

    Germans.
JUST VUNCE A YEAR
VE HAVE A CHANCE TO
  FIND ROMANCE
BENEATH THE DANCE
OF AN ITALIAN LOVER'S
  MOON.
UND VUNCE A YEAR VE
  CAN BE ABSOLUTELY
  FREE
AS IF VE'RE FLOATING
  LIKE A HELIUM
  BALLOON.
BE SURE THERE'S LOTS
  OF IT:
GOOD GERMAN, DAT
  MUSIC.
KEEP IT PLAYING.
KEEP DAT GERMAN
  MUSIC.

UND WAS DU TUST IN
  MEINEM BRUST,
O MEIN GELIEBTER, O
  MEIN HERZ, ALLE
  GELIEBTER, HERZ
  ALLE GELIEB—

    All.
S(H)PA—S(H)PA—S(H)PA—HERE AT THE . . .
(*LITTLE GUIDO runs on and crashes cymbals together.*)
S(H)PA!

(*The number ended, new MUSIC announces LA FLEUR's arrival. LA FLEUR rises ominously and comes forward as GUIDO moves about the spa grounds watching the GERMANS exercising.*)

La Fleur. Contini! Where are you?
Guido. Oh no! (Madame) La Fleur! (*Others clear. GUIDO slinks away. LA FLEUR stalks forward.*)
La Fleur. (*to audience*) All right! So I hear Contini is in Venice, so I come to Venice—I'm paying for this film. I've a right to see it being made, don't you think? I would think. So I go to his room and find a note pinned to the door: "Go to the mud bath." So I go to the mud bath and find a note with my name on it sticking out of the mud: "Go to the steambath." So I go to the steambath. In the steambath I find yet another note! "Go to the garden." (*LA FLEUR freezes, glowering.*)
Guido. (*to the GERMAN WOMEN*) Ah, Frauleins! Tell me, how would you like to be in a film?
German Women. (*together*) Film!
Guido. Ya! Film! Film! Starring roles! All you have to do is give me an *idea* for one! (*GUIDO and GERMANS freeze.*)
La Fleur. (*to audience*) Now I am in the garden and I find still another note! "Go back to the steambath." Well, I have to tell you, I am not pleased with this reception. (*LA FLEUR stalks off, murder in her/his eyes.*)

Scene: THE LOBBY OF THE SPA

(*LUISA is surrounded by REPORTERS.*)

Reporters & Spa People. (*sing*)
NOT SINCE CHARLIE CHAPLIN HAS THERE EVER BEEN A FILM DIRECTOR LIKE THIS—
American Reporter. Mrs. Contini, is there any truth to the rumor that your marriage is in jeopardy?
Luisa. None whatsoever.
Reporters & Spa People. (*sing*)
EVERYTHING HE DOES GETS WORLD ATTENTION—

NINE

BRITISH REPORTER. What about your husband's friendship with Carla Albanese?
LUISA. My husband has many friends.
GERMAN REPORTER. When was the last time he saw Claudia Nardi?
LUISA. I have no idea.
GERMAN REPORTER. Three years ago, in Mallorca—?
LUISA. That was gossip.
BRITISH REPORTER. But in the *public's* mind—
LUISA. Please! When will you understand? (*sings*)
MY HUSBAND MAKES MOVIES.
TO MAKE THEM HE LIVES A KIND OF DREAM
IN WHICH HIS ACTIONS AREN'T ALWAYS WHAT THEY SEEM—
HE MAY BE ON TO SOME UNIQUE ROMANTIC THEME.
SOME MEN CATCH FISH, SOME MEN TIE FLIES,
SOME EARN THEIR LIVING BAKING BREAD.
MY HUSBAND . . . HE GOES A LITTLE CRAZY
MAKING MOVIES INSTEAD.

MY HUSBAND SPINS FANTASIES.
HE LIVES THEM, THEN GIVES THEM TO YOU ALL.
WHILE HE WAS WORKING ON THE FILM ON ANCIENT ROME,
HE MADE THE SLAVE GIRLS TAKE THE GLADIATORS HOME.
SOME MEN BUY STOCKS, SOME MEN PUNCH CLOCKS,
SOME LEAP WHERE OTHERS FEAR TO TREAD.
MY HUSBAND, AS AUTHOR AND DIRECTOR,
MAKES UP STORIES IN HIS HEAD.

(*to herself*)
GUIDO CONTINI, LUISA CONTINI:
NUMBER ONE GENIUS AND NUMBER ONE FAN.
GUIDO CONTINI, LUISA CONTINI:
DAUGHTER OF WELL-TO-DO FLORETINE CLAN
LONG AGO—TWENTY YEARS AGO.
ONCE THE NAMES WERE—
GUIDO CONTINI, LUISA DEL FORNO:
ACTRESS WITH DREAMS AND A LIFE OF HER OWN,
PASSIONATE, WILD AND IN LOVE IN LIVORNO,
SINGING WITH GUIDO ALL NIGHT ON THE PHONE

LONG AGO – SOMEONE ELSE AGO.
HOW HE NEEDS ME SO,
AND HE'LL BE THE LAST TO KNOW IT.

(*to REPORTERS again*)
MY HUSBAND MAKES MOVIES.
TO MAKE THEM HE MAKES HIMSELF OBSESSED.
HE WORKS FOR WEEKS ON END WITHOUT A BIT OF REST –
NO OTHER WAY CAN HE ACHIEVE HIS LEVEL BEST.
SOME MEN READ BOOKS, SOME SHINE THEIR SHOES,
SOME RETIRE EARLY WHEN THEY'VE SEEN THE EVENING NEWS.
MY HUSBAND ONLY RARELY COMES TO BED –
MY HUSBAND MAKES MOVIES INSTEAD.
MY HUSBAND MAKES MOVIES . . .

AMERICAN REPORTER. Thank you very much, Mrs. Contini. (*The song ends, as a flashbulb goes off in LUISA's face. Enter GUIDO.*)

GUIDO. I've got to get out of here! Luisa?

LUISA. I'm in the bedroom.

GUIDO. (*arriving in the bedroom*) Luisa, darling, listen, bad news: Have you tasted the mineral water? I think they pump it out of the Grand Canal. It will make you sick! No wonder people feel better when they leave this place. Which is what I want to do. Right now. Where's the phone book? (*He starts searching for the phone book.*)

LUISA. Guido, by any chance has your producer just arrived?

GUIDO. My producer . . . my producer! Funny you should ask, I just saw her/him in the garden. What a pleasure seeing her/him again!

LUISA. Did you show her/him your script?

GUIDO. (*in despair*) What script?

LUISA. Oh . . . I see . . . Guido, listen, if you had no idea for a film, why'd you sign a contract?

GUIDO. Because she/he *offered* it to me!

CARLA. (*sings*)

GUIDO . . .

GUIDO. (*stands, as if picking up the phone*) Pronto!

OUR LADY OF THE SPA. Signor Contini, telephone. Go ahead.

CARLA. (*sings*)

GUIDO . . .

I WAS LAZING AROUND MY BEDROOM WHEN AN

NINE

IDEA OCCURRED TO ME I THOUGHT YOU MIGHT BE
WONDERING ABOUT, GUIDO . . .

(*NOTE: In the Broadway production, this was a subtly suggestive, highly acrobatic number. Without leaving the vicinity of her box, CARLA gracefully twisted herself into a variety of positions, and at one point even sang while upside down.*)

WHO'S NOT WEARING ANY CLOTHES? I'M NOT!
MY DARLING,
WHO'S AFRAID TO KISS YOUR TOES? I'M NOT!
YOUR MAMA DEAR IS BLOWING INTO YOUR EAR,
SO YOU'LL GET IT LOUD AND CLEAR,
I NEED YOU TO SQUEEZE ME HERE . . .
AND HERE . . .
AND HERE . . .
(*GUIDO seems in pain.*)
    LUISA. Is something wrong?
    GUIDO. What? Oh, I'm not sure. It's about my film. It's from the Vatican. Go ahead, Monsignor.
    CARLA. (*sings*)
COOTCHIE, COOTCHIE, COOTCHIE COO. I'VE GOT
A PLAN FOR WHAT I'M GONNA DO TO YOU, SO HOT
YOU'RE GONNA STEAM, AND SCREAM,
AND VIBRATE LIKE A STRING I'M PLUCKING—
KISS YOUR FEVERED LITTLE BROW,
PINCH YOUR CHEEKS TILL YOU SAY "OW,"
AND I CAN HARDLY WAIT TO SHOW YOU HOW, GUIDO.
WHO WON'T CARE IF YOU COME TO ME TIRED AND
    OVERWORKED?
I WON'T! BAMBINO,
WHO KNOWS A THERAPY TO BEAT WHAT YOU CAN
    GET FROM ME?
I DON'T!
BUT THIS WILL HAVE TO BE ENOUGH FOR NOW,
    GUIDO,
CIAO.
(*speaking*) I love you, Guido. (*The song ends.*)
    LUISA. (*noticing that GUIDO seems stunned*) Guido . . . You've handled the Vatican before.
    GUIDO. The Vatican? . . . Oh yes, the Vatican! But before, the Vatican didn't attack until I'd *finished* a film! What is it about me that the Church doesn't like? What, *what*?

LUISA. Guido, calm down. When are you supposed to start shooting?

GUIDO. What's today?

LUISA. Monday.

GUIDO. Friday. No, I mean really, this is no joke. The crew arrives tomorrow. We're supposed to start building the sets, the props — *what* sets, *what* props? You know something? If I don't come up with a very good idea very quick, my career is finished, done for, kaput! (*An idea strikes.*) A *Western!* (*GUIDO, joined by LITTLE GUIDO, tries out a Western motif with his "orchestra."*)

LUISA. Well, you're in a lot of trouble!

GUIDO. That's not what I needed you to say!

LUISA. What would you *like* me to say?

GUIDO. Say, "Guido, you've been in situations just as tough as this before!"

LUISA. Guido, you've been in situations just as tough as this before!

GUIDO. Really! And how did I get out of them?

LUISA. What's my next line?

GUIDO. I don't know.

LUISA. I don't either.

GUIDO. Oh my God! (*Another idea strikes.*) A Bible epic! (*He and LITTLE GUIDO try out a Bible motif with the "orchestra."*) "Go forth unto that mountain, and there you will find an Academy Award!"

LUISA. What'd you say that made her/him *offer* you this contract?

GUIDO. I can't remember. A documentary? (*He decides to give that a try.*) A documentary!

GUIDO'S ORCHESTRA.
KUMBASA, O GUIDO, KULANUMBAYE!

LUISA. (*She, of course, does not see the orchestra.*) You know what I think?

GUIDO. (*coming out of it*) What?

LUISA. I think you should take the day off.

GUIDO. Luisa, I can't! At this rate, in four days they'll shoot *me!*

LUISA. Guido, no one's going to shoot you. What you need is to *relax.* I know how you work. The ideas have to come of their *own* accord.

GUIDO. What if they don't?

LUISA. Improvise.

NINE

GUIDO. Oh yes. Here's one. How about a film dealing with the last days of a director's once glorious career? It takes place in a spa. At the end he shoots himself.
LUISA. There you are! How simple.
GUIDO. Oh my God!
LUISA. Guido, we came here to relax. Trust me. (*softer, seductive tone*) I've ordered a picnic lunch.
GUIDO. You've what?
LUISA. Olives. Prosciutto. Some cool white wine.
GUIDO. (*touched*) Luisa!
LUISA. And I've rented a gondola for the day. It's enclosed in the middle. With drapes on the windows. I thought we'd just kind of . . . drift around . . . see what comes up.
GUIDO. (*clearly turned on by her*) Oh, Luisa! What would I do without you? (*sings*)
BEING JUST ME IS SO EASY TO BE WHEN I'M ONLY
   WITH YOU—
OPEN INSIDE AND WITH NOTHING TO HIDE FROM
   YOUR VIEW.
SEEMS LONG AGO I WAS DESTINED TO KNOW,
AND THE MOMENT I SAW YOU I KNEW,
I COULD BE TOTALLY HAPPY WITH NO ONE BUT YOU.
   CARLA. (*in GUIDO's mind*) Guido . . .
   GUIDO. Carla! (*sings to her*)
PASSIONATE NIGHT AFTER PASSIONATE NIGHT I
   GIVE OVER TO YOU.
UTTERLY CHANGED, I'M AT EACH PREARRANGED
   RENDEZVOUS.
LURED BY THE FIRE OF YOUR ENDLESS DESIRE,
I STILL WONDER THE WAY THAT IT GREW.
NEVER ELUSIVE, IT COMES FROM EXCLUSIVELY YOU.

FINDING A SPECIAL PERSON WE CAN LOVE IS SO
   RARE—
HOW IN THE WORLD CAN THERE BE TWO?
   CLAUDIA. (*in GUIDO's mind*)
GUIDO . . . !
   GUIDO. Claudia! (*to her*)
SEND ME A LOVE THAT WILL MEND ME WITH LOVE,
I AM DESPERATE FOR YOU,
GIVING YOU CHASE LIKE SOME GODDESS OF GRACE I
   PURSUE.
BLINDED BY NEED, I WILL FOLLOW YOUR LEAD—

MONKEY SEE, MONKEY SAY, MONKEY DO.
TAKEN FOR GRANTED, COMPLETELY ENCHANTED BY
  YOU.

SMALL WONDER IT SEEMS THAT MY LIFE'S MADE OF
  DREAMS
AND OF WISHES THAT NEVER COME TRUE.
I WOULDN'T BE LONELY IF I COULD BE ONLY WITH
  YOU
(*to CARLA*)
... AND YOU ...
(*to LUISA*)
... AND YOU.

Scene: CONFERENCE OF WOMEN
(*GUIDO'S FAN CLUB*)

FIRST WOMAN. The thing about Guido is that he makes you feel like you're the only woman who exists.

SECOND WOMAN. (*without malice*) I ran into him once on Haymarket Street. We'd made love the night before. He just looked at me and said, "Don't I know you?" (*The women laugh, knowingly.*)

THIRD WOMAN. "The Garden of Earthly Delights." That's the first film of his I ever saw. I'd never seen such passion on the screen! When Guido kissed Claudia Nardi, well, I almost fainted! Really. I think it changed my life.

FOURTH WOMAN. I believe that's the first film he ever made. No one had ever made a film like that before. It won the Gold Palm at Cannes and took first prize here at the Venice Film Festival.

FIRST WOMAN. (*with awe*) I remember thinking on seeing it — how beautiful it would be if we could really live in a world like the one Contini had created.

FIFTH WOMAN. (*tearfully; deeply moved*) It was filled with such magic — such wonderment!

SIXTH WOMAN. (*lovingly*) We were lovers once, for almost a month. I never knew anyone who seemed to need me so much.

(*Lights fade on the WOMEN, as lights up on OUR LADY OF THE SPA.*)

OUR LADY OF THE SPA. We were sitting by the fountain at the spa. For a long while he said nothing, just stared into the water.

Then all at once he turned and said, "What am I to do?" And I said, without hesitation, "You must *choose*."

Scene: LA FLEUR'S SUITE AT THE SPA

Guido. As I see it, if we were to shoot the script I have, we would make maybe a one- or two-million-dollar profit. HOWEVER! If we delay till winter—snow! ice! —it's the environment this film really needs! We're talking ten, twelve million profit. Think it over. I myself can live with the delay.

La Fleur. No delay. One million profit is just fine.

Guido. (*glumly*) Right.

La Fleur. So. Now. Could you please show me the script?

Guido. Unfortunately, I work in a kind of shorthand. If I were to show you what I've done, it would look like a . . . a . . . shopping list.

La Fleur. I see.

Guido. But then this is how I work.

La Fleur. Your last three films were flops.

Guido. That's only because no one came.

La Fleur. (*not amused*) Contini, listen. I have advanced you a huge amount of money. If you are not ready when the crew arrives, not only will I sue you, but I shall see that you never work again. (*GUIDO chuckles.*) Lina/Leo, darling, tell him what I did to that designer who double-crossed me when I owned the Folies Bergeres. (*LINA/LEO whispers to GUIDO. He is aghast.*) So. Now. Who do you have in the cast?

Guido. Well, so far, just these four Germans. Very talented, I think. And of course, *I must have Claudia Nardi!* (*CLAUDIA comes to him, lies across his lap, seen only by him.*) She's really crucial to this project. A vast audience is out there waiting! Hoping! PRAYING! for us to be reunited again . . . On the screen, I mean.

La Fleur. I talked to Claudia in Paris. She told me she will not do your film unless you show her the script first.

Guido. Yes, well . . . (*CLAUDIA starts stroking him.*) . . . if she would just come to Venice . . . (*to CLAUDIA*) . . . Now is not a good time for this.

La Fleur. What?

Guido. (*back to reality*) If she would just come to Venice! (*CLAUDIA starts stroking him again.*) I could describe her role for her. That's much better than seeing the script. (*to CLAUDIA*) Stop! STOP! (*CLAUDIA moves away.*)

LA FLEUR. Contini, are you all right?
GUIDO. Of course.
LA FLEUR. . . . So there really *is* a script?
GUIDO. Absolutely.
LA FLEUR. Good. From now on, you will work on it with my new associate producer, Stephanie/Stefan Necrophorus. She/He writes for *Cahier du Cinema* under the name Robespierre.
NECROPHORUS. Kyrie Contini.
GUIDO. So *you* are Robespierre!
NECROPHORUS. I am not an admirer of yours.
GUIDO. I've gathered.
LA FLEUR. I thought she/he would bring some objectivity to the project. (*to NECROPHORUS*) Tell him what you think of his work.
NECROPHORUS. I find it visually stunning, but emotionally inane.
LA FLEUR. You see how helpful she's/he's going to be?
GUIDO. It's staggering.
NECROPHORUS. Now. If you would please tell me what your new film is about, perhaps I can help you with its plot, which has always been one of your weakest points.
GUIDO. Right. Thank you, that's very generous. Let me see, where do I begin? (*He ponders.*) At first . . . *nothing*. (*He ponders more.*) Then . . . music! (*He sings.*)
THE ACTION BEGINS IN A GRAVEYARD.
A MAN HAS BEEN BURIED ALIVE.
HE'S SCRATCHING AND CLAWING.
POOR FELLOW, HE'S CAUGHT IN A TERRIBLE
 CRUNCH!

HE'S FIGHTING HIS WAY TO THE SURFACE.
IT'S LIKELY HE'LL NEVER SURVIVE.
HE HARDLY CAN BREATHE,
AND HE'S DESPERATE TO KEEP AN APPOINTMENT
 FOR LUNCH.
LA FLEUR. An appointment for lunch? That's absurd!
GUIDO. It's *humorous!*
LA FLEUR. It sounds depressing.
GUIDO. It does. (*sings*)
IN FACT WE BEGIN WITH A WEDDING,
A PROLOGUE TO WHAT I'VE DESCRIBED.
WE'RE HAPPY AND GAY AND IN LOVE AND IT'S SPRING
AND THE TREES ARE ALL GREEN.

A TRIO OF CAPUCHIN MONKEYS
INSINUATES INTO THE FRAME.
THEY CHATTER A BIT AND THEN ONE DISAPPEARS,
BUT THE OTHERS REMAIN . . .
HAVE I MENTIONED THE TRAIN?
   LA FLEUR. Train?
   GUIDO. Of course! There are trains in all Contini films! It's my signature! (*sings*)
WITH A BOLD CLEAN MASTERSTROKE,
A BOLD CLEAN MASTERSTROKE,
SUDDENLY, SUDDENLY, SUDDENLY, SUDDENLY,
SUDDENLY WE SEE FIRE AND SMOKE.
WITH A BOLD CLEAN MASTERSTROKE,
A BOLD CLEAN MASTERSTROKE,
SUDDENLY, SUDDENLY, SUDDENLY, SUDDENLY,
SUDDENLY THERE'S A TRAIN!

WITH A BOLD CLEAN MASTERSTROKE,
A BOLD CLEAN MASTERSTROKE,
SUDDENLY, SUDDENLY, SUDDENLY, SUDDENLY,
SUDDENLY ONE COLOSSAL JOKE!
AND THE MONKEYS ALL GET ON,
THE MONKEYS ALL GET ON,
SUDDENLY, SUDDENLY, SUDDENLY, SUDDENLY,
SUDDENLY THEY'RE ALL GONE!
Ciao! (*He tries to leave.*)
   LA FLEUR. (*calling him back*) Contini! This is not what I want! There are no trains in a spa. There are no monkeys in a spa. And where is le singing? Where is le dansing?
   GUIDO. What singing? What dancing?
   LA FLEUR. When we had lunch in Paris, you told me you couldn't *wait* to do a musical!
   GUIDO. A *musical*?
   LA FLEUR. Why do you think I gave you this contract?
   GUIDO. What was I drinking at this lunch?
   LA FLEUR. (*outdone, enraged*) Mais c'est pas possible! Je n'en peux plus! Pourquoi faut-il que je m'associe toujours avec les idiots? Madonna, madonna! (*sings*)
LE CINEMA TODAY IS IN A CRISIS.
DIRECTORS ARE SO EXISTENTIALISTES.
THE MOVIES ARE NOT WORTH THEIR ENTRANCE
   PRICES
IF NO ONE SINGS A LOVE SONG WHEN HE'S KISSED.

(*speaks*) Contini! I want a musical! (*sings*)
LOVE CANNOT BE LOVE WITHOUT LE SINGING,
A STRING, A CLARINET, A SAXOPHONE.
TAKE A LESSON FROM THIS OLD PARISIAN
AND THE FINEST ENTERTAINMENT SHE/HE HAS KNOWN.

FOLIES BERGERES —
WHAT A SHOWING OF COLOR, COSTUME, AND DANCING!
NOT A MOMENT IN LIFE COULD BE MORE ENTRANCING
THAN AN EVENING YOU SPEND AUX FOLIES BERGERES.
FOLIES BERGERES,
NOT A SOUL IN THE WORLD COULD BE IN DESPAIR
WHEN HE IS GLANCING
AT THE FABULOUS STAGE DES FOLIES BERGERES.

THINK OF THE FOOTLIGHTS BRIGHT AND GLEAMING,
LE STRIP-TEASE, LE CAN-CAN WE ALL ADORE.
LIFE IS TOO SHORT WITHOUT DREAMING,
AND DREAMS ARE WHAT LE CINEMA IS FOR.

FOLIES BERGERES —
LA MUSIQUE ET LA DANSE, LE SON, LA LUMIERE!
LES PETITS JOLIS SEINS DES BELLES BOUQUETIERES
SUR LA BELLE PASSERELLE DES FOLIES BERGERES.
PAS DE MYSTERE —
LE SPECTACLE EST TOUT A FAIT DECOUVERT.

(*NOTE: What follows is a section of LILIANE LA FLEUR's passerelle monologue from the original Broadway production of NINE. It is provided solely to demonstrate how one LA FLEUR was able to recreate for GUIDO the intimacy, charm, and warmth of the Folies Bergeres. The passerelle routine is improvisatory and must be tailored to the talents of the performer playing LA FLEUR. It is optional and can easily be excised from the number.*)

(*LA FLEUR goes to GUIDO and whispers in his ear. He nods and announces.*)

NINE

GUIDO. Mesdames et messieurs! Et maintenant—la vedette des Folies Bergeres: Liliane La Fleur!

LA FLEUR. (*crossing onto the passerelle and speaking to the audience*) Bon soir. Je suis la vedette des Folies Bergeres a Paris, et ca, c'est la passerelle de mon souvenir. Passerelle . . . it's a runway . . . did you know that? Anyway, I have to tell you, I have received before the show a HUGE bouquet of roses, and the person who sent it to me is here tonight. And I would like to thank him. Who is it? (*to some man in the audience*) Hello, there. Did you do it? Did you send me the flowers? . . . Why not? I have to find out who did it. (*to another man*) Did you send me the flowers? Don't ask her, I'm talking to you. . . . You did? Oh that's great! What is your name? . . . Jerry? You're a liar. That's not the name on the card. (*LITTLE GUIDO has appeared before her, holding a small gift box behind him.*) What are you doing here? This is the stage of the Folies Bergeres. You're too young to be here. You're too young or you're too short. Does this child belong to anyone? Please? Because I don't know what to do with you, I really—You don't understand a word I'm saying, do you? You're not an American? (*He shakes his head.*) Oh, I see . . . Are you French? (*He shakes his head.*) Well, nobody's perfect. Are you Italian? (*He nods.*) I knew it! Moi aussi: la moitie francaise, la—(*He turns, revealing the gift box.*) I don't believe this. He brought me a gift. Did you bring this all the way from Italy? Is this cheese? Formaggio? Merci, cheri. Now you go home, my sweetheart. (*He starts off.*) Wait a minute! Bambino! Vieni a chi—a qui—or whatever. (*He returns.*) In the other hand, you can wait for me in my dressing room. I will see you after the show. (*He runs off.*) Well he's Italian, isn't he? (*NECROPHORUS steps forward.*)

NECROPHORUS. (*sings*)
THE TROUBLE WITH CONTINI, HE'S THE KING OF
   MEDIOCRITIES,
A SECOND-RATE DIRECTOR WHO BELIEVES THAT HE
   IS SOCRATES.
HE NEVER MAKES A "MOVIE" OR A "PICTURE" OR A
   "FLICK"
HE MAKES A "FILM"—GET IT?—A "FILM".

A TYPICAL ITALIAN WITH HIS AUTO AND BIOGRAPHY,
A MIXTURE OF CATHOLICISM, PASTA, AND
   PORNOGRAPHY,

A SUPERFICIAL, WOMANIZING, MODERATELY CHARMING LATIN FRAUD.
  Guido.
GRAZIE!
  Necrophorus.
PREGO!
AND WHAT ARE HIS MOVIES ABOUT?
JUST BEAUTY, TRUTH, DEATH, YOUTH, LOVE, LIFE, ANGUISH, ANGST.
THANKS TO HIM WE HAVE BOREDOM AT THE MOVIES.
  Guido.
GRAZIE!
  Necrophorus.
PREGO!
  La Fleur. (*reclaiming spotlight*)
DARLINGS!

La Fleur.	Necrophorus.	Others.
FOLIES BER-GERES—	THE TROUBLE WITH CONTINI, HE'S THE KING OF MEDIOCRATES, A	OOH LA
LA MUSIQUE ET LA DANSE, LE SON, LA LUMIERE!	SECOND-RATE DIRECTOR WHO BELIEVES THAT HE IS SOCRATES. HE NEVER MAKES A MOVIE OR A PICTURE OR A FLICK, HE MAKES A	LA OOH LA
LES PETITS JOLIS SEINS DES BELLES BOUQUETIERES.	FILM— GET IT? — A FILM. A TYPICAL ITALIAN WITH HIS AUTO AND BIOGRAPHY, A	LA OOH LA
SUR LA BELLE PASSERELLE DES FOLIES	MIXTURE OF CATHOLICISM, PASTA, AND PORNOGRAPHY, A	LA

NINE

BERGERES.	SUPERFICIAL, WOMANIZING,	OOH
	MODERATELY CHARMING LATIN	LA
PAS DE MYSTERE—	FRAUD.	LA
	AND WHAT ARE HIS	OOH
	MOVIES ABOUT? JUST	LA
LE SPECTACLE EST TOUT A FAIT DECOUVERT.	BEAUTY, TRUTH, DEATH, YOUTH,	LA
	LOVE, LIFE,	OOH
	ANGUISH, ANGST.	LA
ET PAS TROP CHER.	THANKS TO HIM WE HAVE BOREDOM AT THE MOVIES.	LA
		OOH
		LA
		LA
VIENS CE SOIR AVEC MOI AUX FOLIES BERGERES!	VIENS CE SOIR AVEC MOI AUX FOLIES BERGERES!	

(*NOTE: The following instrument music may be used to accompany a boa dance, as in the original Broadway production; a dance for LA FLEUR and COMPANY sans boa; or may be cut entirely. What follows is the Broadway version.*)

(*LA FLEUR opens the gift box and pulls out one end of a feather boa that she eventually trails over forty-six feet of passerelle.*)

LA FLEUR. I love it! (*She dances with the boa, wrapping herself in it. A waltz, then all join in a can-can.*)
ALL.
FOLIES BERGERES—
THE MUSIC, THE LIGHTS, AND THE LAUGHTER,
THE ANSWER TO WHAT YOU ARE AFTER
EACH NIGHT AT THE FOLIES BERGERES.
FOLIES BERGERES—

La Fleur. (*to GUIDO*)
TO YOUR MODERN IDEAS I SIMPLY COMPARE
ONE DERRIERE
  All.
AT THE FOLIES BERGERES!
THE ANSWER TO WHAT YOU ARE AFTER,
THE MUSIC, THE LIGHTS, AND THE LAUGHTER
OF THE FOLIES BERGERES!

La Fleur. So! There you are! This is what I want!
Guido. You're joking.
La Fleur. No, I'm not joking! When you signed the contract, you signed to do a musical! I want le singing! I want le dansing! I want a musical! Do it!

(*BLACKOUT*)

Scene: IN THE CATACOMBS OF THE SPA

Our Lady of the Spa. Signor Contini, His Eminence has granted your request for an interview . . . It's the oldest part of the spa. Rumor has it that several saints are buried in these catacombs. It offers the Cardinal the kind of privacy he needs when he comes for the baths . . . Don't stay too long; he isn't well. Your Eminence, Signor Contini is here. (*GUIDO reads both his own lines and the CARDINAL's.*)
Guido. I am very grateful for you granting me this visit.
Cardinal. What can I do for you, my son?
Guido. Do you believe in God?
Cardinal. (*taken aback*) Excuse me, are you a Catholic?
Guido. Oh yes. Very much so. Not as much as I would like to be, or as much as *you* would like me to be, I'm sure. But I'm certainly trying.
Cardinal. Try harder.
Guido. Well, I don't know how! Father, look, I'm confused. I've reached a point in my life where I don't know which way to turn anymore. And it's affecting me in peculiar ways. (*A church bell rings.*) Father, I have been seeing things of late—people, visions. Sometimes they remind me of my early days in school, and I think that what I'm seeing must be the work of the Devil. (*A NUN and FOUR BOYS pass in the background.*)
Cardinal. My son. If you can believe in a world in which you

NINE

can see the Devil, surely you must also believe in a world in which you can see an angel. (*The NUN and BOYS exit. GUIDO'S MOTHER rises.*)

GUIDO. Mama . . .
GUIDO'S MOTHER. (*sings*)
GUIDO . . .
GUIDO'S AUNTS. (*sing*)
GUIDO . . .
GUIDO'S MOTHER. (*sings*)
CARO MIO . . .
GUIDO'S AUNTS. (*sing*)
CARO MIO . . .
GUIDO'S MOTHER.
TIME TO COME OUT OF YOUR BATH,
WRAP YOU UP IN A MOTHER'S LOVE,
TAKE A TOWEL AND DRY YOUR LITTLE HEAD.
GUIDO'S MOTHER & AUNTS.
TIME TO COME OUT IN THE AIR,
SLEEPY PUP IN YOUR MOTHER'S ARMS,
PLANT A KISS ON YOUR LIPS AND PUT YOU TO BED.

NINE, GUIDO!
HAPPY BIRTHDAY TO YOU.
NINE, GUIDO.
SO MUCH TO DO!

TIME TO START OUT ON YOUR OWN,
OPEN UP TO A BRAND NEW WORLD,
TIME TO LEAVE EARLY DREAMS AND LIVE THEM
  INSTEAD.

GUIDO'S MOTHER & ONE AUNT.
NINE, GUIDO.
GUIDO'S MOTHER.
NINE MONTHS OF THE YEAR TO MAKE YOU APPEAR.
GUIDO'S MOTHER & AUNTS.
NINTH IN A FAMILY OF NINE,
ONE AUNT.
NINTH GRANDCHILD,
GUIDO'S MOTHER.
NINTH SON—
GUIDO'S MOTHER & AUNTS.
NINTH . . . BUT NUMBER ONE.

TIME TO COME OUT OF YOUR EGG,
CRACK IT OPEN AND SHOW YOUR FACE.
(*As GUIDO has moved into the lap of LUISA, the AUNTS have wrapped LITTLE GUIDO and placed him into the lap of MAMA.*)
DON'T CONCEAL WHAT YOU FEEL,
LET IT SHINE:
THAT YOU'D LIKE TO BE ALWAYS NINE.
(*Blackout. Lights up on CARLA.*)

CARLA. Guido, this is just not my idea of a successful relationship! Four days I've been here now, and you haven't come to see me once. I thought you loved me.

GUIDO. (*half asleep in LUISA's lap*) I do. I do!

CARLA. Well, obviously not enough. I think I'm going to kill myself.

GUIDO. (*suddenly awake*) No! No! I'll be right over! (*rising*) Luisa, darling, listen, I'm going out for a while. Clear my head. Maybe some ideas will—

LUISA. *Clothes.*

GUIDO. What?

LUISA. Bring her some clothes.

GUIDO. Bring *who* some clothes?

LUISA. Carla. Isn't that who called you before?

GUIDO. *Carla?* . . . No! Whatever gave you such an idea? I told you, that's all over with . . . Anyway, why would I want to bring her some clothes?

LUISA. So when you're seen with her, she won't look so . . . *tacky.*

GUIDO. You think she looks "tacky"?

LUISA. But perhaps that's what you like.

GUIDO. Now wait a second!

LUISA. Look, I think you'd better hurry. Maybe this time she really *will* kill herself.

GUIDO. *What are you talking about?*

LUISA. Guido, I don't think you've been to see her since we got here. Which means she must be due for another suicide threat.

GUIDO. You really think she's here.

LUISA. Well maybe I'm wrong.

GUIDO. Yes, *very* wrong! You do me a terrible disservice! I can't believe this lack of trust! I'm really staggered! If you'll excuse me, I'm going out! (*MUSIC. A samba beat, as GUIDO runs to CARLA's embrace.*)

CARLA. I just love the clothes you brought me!

NINE

GUIDO. Ohhh, I'm so relieved! I hope it will make up for my not having been here.

CARLA. No, I don't think so.

GUIDO. Carla. Carlissima!

CARLA. No, get away. Don't touch me, don't try to make up with me. I'm very upset with you.

GUIDO. But darling! Angel of fire, light of my loins! Don't you think I'd have been here if I *could* have?

CARLA. What did she do? Have you followed?

GUIDO. This is not Luisa's fault! I've been working on a film. If I don't come up with an idea for it by tomorrow, guess what my producer has sworn she/he will do to me? (*He whispers to her. She stares at his groin aghast.*) So, you see, in a way I am working here for *both* of us. (*She laughs, falls on him as they wrestle to the floor.*) Now why don't you go and try on what I've brought? Maybe it'll give me an idea for a film—who knows?—stranger things have happened. I'm very desperate. Hurry, I don't have much time. Tomorrow rapidly approaches. Please! (*A church bell rings.*)

GUIDO'S MOTHER. (*to LUISA from another part of the stage*) Luisa darling. There's something I've been meaning to ask you.

CARLA. (*crawling away from GUIDO*) You still haven't asked me about my news.

GUIDO'S MOTHER. (*continuing to LUISA*) But how do you put up with Guido?

GUIDO. (*to CARLA*) What news?

GUIDO'S MOTHER. (*to LUISA*) Not that Guido isn't wonderful!

CARLA. (*still crawling away*) The news I came to Venice to tell you about!

GUIDO. What news is that?

LUISA. (*to GUIDO's MOTHER*) Guido's in a lot of trouble.

CARLA. (*seeing that GUIDO's mind is elsewhere*) I'll tell you later—when you're more interested.

(*A church bell rings. GUIDO, kneeling, clasps his hands in prayer. CARLA leaves as a NUN passes in the background, followed by four BOYS, LITTLE GUIDO among them. The WOMEN begin humming a Gregorian Chant.*)

CARLA. (*from offstage, ecstatically*) Oh, Guido! Whatever made you think of getting me this? It's very sexy! I've never worn anything like this in my life! I think you could be excommunicated for getting me a thing like this!

GUIDO. I'm glad you like it. (*The NUN onstage begins to walk through the double scene, unnoticed.*)

GUIDO'S MOTHER. (*to LUISA*) I left Guido's father once, you know. Hardest thing I ever did. Worst year of my life. Not something I would recommend.

CARLA. I just wish I could wear this out in public!

GUIDO'S MOTHER. (*to LUISA*) But sometimes you have no choice. (*The NUN passes GUIDO.*)

GUIDO. Actually, I was thinking you could wear it when you're out with me. (*The NUN smacks GUIDO's head.*)

CARLA. (*still offstage*) Guido, you're a genius!

GUIDO. Thank you.

CARLA. With me in this, we can be seen *anywhere* together!

GUIDO. I know. What a couple!

GUIDO'S MOTHER. (*to LUISA*) Afterwards we got back together, it was better . . . I think. (*The NUN walking through the scene has discarded her habit, revealing herself as SARRAGHINA, a voluptuous whore.*)

CARLA. (*entering in a nun's habit*) Hail Carla, full of grace!

GUIDO. (*looking at CARLA with awe and lust*) Oh my God! (*In the background, ONE of the FOUR BOYS returns to seek a hole in the fence. It is LITTLE GUIDO.*)

GUIDO'S MOTHER. (*to LUISA*) By the way, in case you're curious: I know where Guido's problems began.

GUIDO. (*as CARLA walks before him, nunlike*) Yes . . . yes. Good!

GUIDO'S MOTHER. Maybe if I hadn't sent him to that parochial school!

GUIDO. Come on! Let's go to the beach to see Sarraghina! (*The OTHER BOYS run to LITTLE GUIDO*—"Sarraghina!" "Sh!" *They begin crawling through the hole in the fence.*)

GUIDO'S MOTHER. But how was I to know? We were hoping he would be a priest, you see. (*Both CARLA and SARRAGHINA are walking before GUIDO.*)

GUIDO. Now stop. (*CARLA and SARRAGHINA obey.*) Turn around. (*They both obey.*) Lower your head. (*CARLA lowers her head as SARRAGHINA raises hers.*) Modesty. Shyness. Innocence. Yes, that's it!

GUIDO'S MOTHER. But the school was near this beach. (*SARRAGHINA mimes sprinkling sand.*)

GUIDO. There is something I would like you to tell me.

CARLA & SARRAGHINA. (*together*) What is that, my son?

NINE

GUIDO. Tell me about love! (*The FOUR BOYS start crawling through the scene.*)

SARRAGHINA. So, you little Italian devils, you want to know about love? Sarraghina, she will tell you!

CARLA. My news is that Luigi has agreed to give me a divorce! Oh, Guido! That means all you have to do is get *your* divorce, and then we're free to marry! Luigi's lawyer is sending me a letter that will make everything official! Well, what do you think?

GUIDO. (*paying attention only to SARRAGHINA*) I think this is how God meant life to be! (*CARLA exits the scene joyfully, thinking GUIDO is approving of her news. GUIDO, in another world, smiles, crawls like the BOYS to watch SARRAGHINA.*)

SARRAGHINA. (*echoed by GUIDO & BOYS; sings*)
YOU NEVER SAY "I LOVE YOU," IT'S TOO ENGLISH.
DON'T LOVE LIKE THE INGLESI. (NOT THE INGLESI)
AND NEVER SAY "JE T'AIME," IT'S TOO PRETTY.
IT'S GOOD FOR THE FRANCESI. (FOR THE FRANCESI)
IN DUTCH THEY SAY "ICK LIEBE," THEY CAN KEEP IT
WITH ALL THE HOLLANDESI. (THE HOLLANDESI)
BUT NOW I TEACH YOU THREE WORDS, YOU WILL
  LEARN THEM
AND DRIVE YOUR WOMEN CRAZY:

"TI VOGLIO BENE" YOU WILL SAY, IT MEANS "I WANT
  YOU EVERY DAY"—
"TI VOGLIO BENE." (TI VOGLIO BENE)
"TI VOGLIO BENE" YOU WILL LEARN MEANS "EVERY
  NIGHT FOR YOU I BURN"—
"TI VOGLIO BENE." (TI VOGLIO BENE)
NOW WHEN YOU GROW TO BE A MAN, YOU FOLLOW
  SARRAGHINA'S PLAN:
"TI VOGLIO BENE." (TI VOGLIO BENE)
REMEMBER HOW I TAUGHT YOU FIRST THESE WORDS
  OF LOVE THAT WE REHEARSED:
"TI VOGLIO BENE." (TI VOGLIO BENE)
SARRAGHINA.
BUT LOVE IS MORE THAN SPEAKING,
WHEN YOUR SPEAKING IS ALL THROUGH—
COME HERE A LITTLE CLOSER,
I WILL TELL YOU WHAT TO DO . . .
(*The BOYS edge closer. She holds one, then speaks.*) You close your eyes. And if you want to make a woman happy, you rely on

46   NINE

what you were born with. Because it is in your blood. (*She puts the BOY on her lap and sings to him.*)
BE ITALIAN, BE ITALIAN,
TAKE A CHANCE AND TRY TO STEAL A FIERY KISS.
BE ITALIAN, YOU RAPSCALLION.
WHEN YOU HOLD ME, DON'T JUST HOLD ME
BUT HOLD THIS!
(*She puts his hand on her breast. The BOYS all giggle. She sings to LITTLE GUIDO.*)
PLEASE BE GENTLE, SENTIMENTAL,
GO AHEAD AND TRY TO GIVE MY CHEEK A PAT.
(*LITTLE GUIDO pats her cheek; she embraces him.*)
BUT BE DARING AND UNCARING.
WHEN YOU PINCH ME, TRY TO PINCH ME WHERE THERE'S FAT.
(*She pinches his bottom. He runs, turns to listen. Echoed by BOYS:*)
BE A SINGER! (BE A SINGER)
BE A LOVER! (BE A LOVER)
PICK THE FLOWER NOW BEFORE THE CHANCE IS PAST. (BEFORE THE CHANCE IS PAST)
BE ITALIAN, (BE ITALIAN)
YOU RAPSCALLION! (YOU RAPSCALLION)
LIVE TODAY AS IF IT MAY BECOME YOUR LAST!
(*She catches a tambourine thrown from the orchestra pit, and shaking it, leads the BOYS across "the beach", cheered by the PEOPLE on stage.*) Bambini! Ascoltate! Adesso vincerete la tarantella—la danza la piu bella del mondo! La danza che risveglia la passione e l'amore! A posto, bambini! Siete pronti? Attenti! Via! (*English translation:* Kids! Listen up! Now you'll learn the tarantella—the most beautiful dance in the world! The dance that awakens passion and love! To your places! Ready? Set! Go!) (*Sitting on GUIDO's box, she teaches them a tambourine "dance," in which she uses the tambourine to slap various parts of her body—an earthy anatomy lesson. The boys, seated on surrounding boxes, join one by one, building to a wild, infectious climax. Then ALL break into song. Echoed by ALL:*)
BE A SINGER! (BE A SINGER)
BE A LOVER! (BE A LOVER)
PICK THE FLOWER NOW BEFORE THE CHANCE IS PASSED. (AHHHHH)
BE ITALIAN, (BE ITALIAN)

NINE

YOU RAPSCALLION! (YOU RAPSCALLION)
LIVE TODAY AS IF IT MAY BECOME YOUR LAST!

(*The BOYS embrace SARRAGHINA, then run back to the hole in the fence, where their NUN reprimands them for running off to SARRAGHINA. During this, GUIDO's MOTHER has been speaking.*)

GUIDO'S MOTHER. I still don't know how it could have happened—*nine years old!* My son goes to see a woman like that! Father Manfredi told me lots of the boys from St. Sebastian's went to see her. Father Manfredi said she was the Devil!

LITTLE GUIDO. (*receiving smack from NUN*) I didn't know! I didn't know!

(*During the following music, CARLA, still dressed as a nun, ushers the BOYS back on stage, where they clasp their hands in prayer. CARLA moves to SARRAGHINA's box and prays there, having assumed the posture of a nun; SARRAGHINA moves to CARLA's box, sits, and waits.*)

GUIDO. (*sings*)
I REMEMBER ST. SEBASTIAN WITH A MEMORY MOST
  UNKIND.
I CAN HEAR THE BELLS I HEARD WHEN I WENT THERE
INSIDE THE CHURCH, INSIDE MY MIND.

THE BELLS OF ST. SEBASTIAN ONLY RING ONCE IN
  YOUR EARS,
BUT IF YOU'RE VERY YOUNG WHEN YOU HEAR THEM,
THEIR SOUND CAN LAST A HUNDRED YEARS.
  ALL.
BUT THE MUSIC OF THE RINGING
WAS THE MUSIC OF OUR SINGING
WHEN WE WERE SINGING KYRIE ELEISON, KYRIE
  ELEISON, KYRIE ELEISON.
  GUIDO. (*echoed by ALL*)
EACH DAY AT LAUDS, (EACH DAY AT LAUDS)
EACH NIGHT AT VESPERS, (EACH NIGHT AT VESPERS)
FROM EVERY TOWER THE HOUR WOULD BE TOLLED
FOR THOSE OF US AT ST. SEBASTIAN,
NO LONGER YOUNG AND NOT YET OLD.

GUIDO'S MOTHER. But why did you go to this woman?
LITTLE GUIDO. To see what she was like!
GUIDO.
EACH DAY AT ST. SEBASTIAN IN THE CLASSROOM WE WOULD HEAR
THAT DEVILS LURKED BEHIND EVERY CORNER.
IF YOU TRIED TO LOOK, THEY WOULD DISAPPEAR.

THE NUNS OF ST. SEBASTIAN TRIED TO TEACH THE FACTS OF LIFE,
EXPLAINING THERE ARE TWO KINDS OF WOMEN—
ONE WAS A WHORE, ONE WAS A WIFE.
ALL.
BUT THE MUSIC OF THE RINGING
WAS A DIFFERENT WORLD THAT OPENED THROUGH OUR SINGING
WHEN WE WERE SINGING KYRIE ELEISON, KYRIE ELEISON, KYRIE ELEISON.
GUIDO. (*echoed by* ALL)
THEY RANG AT DAWN (THEY RANG AT DAWN)
THEY RANG AT MIDNIGHT (THEY RANG AT MIDNIGHT)
IN TONES WELL-ROUNDED THEY SOUNDED DOWN THE NAVE
FOR ALL THE SOULS OF LITTLE BOYS AT ST. SEBASTIAN
TOO YOUNG TO SAVE.
ALL.
KYRIE ELEISON, ELEISON, CHRISTE ELEISON, ELEISON.
GUIDO'S MOTHER. You've brought such shame on us!
LITTLE GUIDO. But Mama, I didn't know!
ALL.
FOR LUNCH AT ST. SEBASTIAN, COUNTRY CHEESE AND BUTTERED BREAD,
GUIDO.
A PRAYER WE NEVER LEARNED SUNG IN LATIN,
THEN A MIDDAY NAP IN A MAKESHIFT BED,
ALL.
THEN THE MUSIC OF THE RINGING,
THEN THE MUSIC OF OUR SINGING,
AND WE WERE SINGING KYRIE ELEISON, KYRIE ELEISON, KYRIE ELEISON.

Guido. (*echoed by ALL*)
WE SHOULD HAVE KNOWN. (WE SHOULD HAVE
  KNOWN)
THEY SHOULD HAVE WARNED US. (THEY SHOULD
  HAVE WARNED US)
AT ST. SEBASTIAN THEY NEVER SPARED THE ROD,
  (AT ST. SEBASTIAN THEY NEVER SPARED THE ROD)
  Guido.
BUT IN THE MUSIC OF THE BELLS AT ST. SEBASTIAN
WE LOOKED FOR GOD.
  Little Guido.
KYRIE ELEISON . . . (*As the MUSIC continues, LITTLE
GUIDO steals away and starts running.*)
  Guido's Mother. Guido, where are you running to?

(*LITTLE GUIDO has run back to wave at SARRAGHINA.
  She returns his wave as the curtain falls to end Act One.*)

ACT TWO

Lights up on the same stage picture that ended Act One. We are on a beach, somewhere in Venice. It is dusk. CLAUDIA rises.

CLAUDIA. Guido, I've just flown in from Paris. I am extremely tired, hungry, cold. Why have you brought me to this beach?
GUIDO. (*abstracted*) What?
CLAUDIA. Guido, where is my hotel? (*OTHERS begin slowly to exit.*)
GUIDO. Oh. I'll drive you there in a minute. But first I thought you'd like to see this beach. An extraordinary woman once danced for me on a beach like this.
CLAUDIA. Is that the woman I'm supposed to play in your film?
GUIDO. No. No-no!
CLAUDIA. Then why'd you think I'd want to see this beach?
GUIDO. Well I just thought you'd be interested. God, I love it when it's cold like this! The wind whipping in off the Adriatic! You really feel it! Right down to the bone!
CLAUDIA. (*shivering*) Yes. It's a wonderful feeling. Guido, who do I play in this film?
GUIDO. A woman who heals.
CLAUDIA. (*disappointed*) You mean like a nurse?
GUIDO. No, nothing like a nurse! Nurses heal the flesh! You . . . you . . .
CLAUDIA. I know. I heal the *spirit*.
GUIDO. Yes, that's it!
CLAUDIA. And how do I do this?
GUIDO. Well with, with . . .
CLAUDIA. Sorcery!
GUIDO. Exactly! God, I can't believe how suited you are for this role! I can see you in it now!
CLAUDIA. Guido, this is the part I played in "The Garden of Earthly Delights."
GUIDO. Yes, well, that was a long time ago. And let me remind you, it was a very big hit! Visconti never had a hit like that!
CLAUDIA. It's also the role I played in "Cathedral of Dreams."
GUIDO. An even bigger hit.
CLAUDIA. And in "Via Veneto."
GUIDO. Biggest hit of all! You see? This role is made for you!
CLAUDIA. I don't want to play it anymore.

GUIDO. But you've got to! I haven't had a hit like those in years!

CLAUDIA. Of course you have.

GUIDO. No-no, not really. My last three have been outright flops. Producers are not exactly knocking down my door. I've lost something, I don't know what. But I know you can help me find it.

CLAUDIA. Inspiration.

GUIDO. Yes!

CLAUDIA. Guido, I was never your inspiration. That's what you imagine, but it was always you. I can't play this role for you anymore.

GUIDO. This role made you a star!

CLAUDIA. Guido, I am not a spirit. I am real. I have a life you know nothing about. And have never shown the slightest interest in. I shouldn't have come here.

GUIDO. So why did you? . . . You came because I understand you like no other person does.

CLAUDIA. You don't understand me at all!

GUIDO. That just shows how much you know about yourself.

CLAUDIA. Guido, you have invented me! No such person exists!

GUIDO. In my mind, she exists! On the screen, she exists! And now, everywhere, in people's dreams, *she exists.*

CLAUDIA. I came because Luisa asked me to come.

GUIDO. . . . What?

CLAUDIA. Luisa. She called me in Paris. She said she didn't think she could help you anymore. She thought maybe I could. Well, I can't.

GUIDO. Look, I'll change the role. You'll play a different role.

CLAUDIA. It wouldn't work.

GUIDO. Why not?

CLAUDIA. Because I can't go through this kind of relationship with you again. It takes too much out of me. And Luisa is your wife. Excuse me, I'm going back to the car. (*She starts off.*)

GUIDO. Claudia, I love you!

CARLA. (*stopping; to herself*) Oh my God.

GUIDO. It's true. And you know it's true. Why are you laughing?

CLAUDIA. I'm not laughing.

GUIDO. I can see your back moving up and down. Of course you're laughing! My life's falling apart, my career is crumbling, I

tell you that I love you, and you're standing there laughing. . . !
   Claudia. (*sings*)
A MAN LIKE YOU
ONE WOMAN'S NOT ENOUGH FOR YOU, GUIDO.
   Guido.
ONE'S PLENTY IF SHE'S YOU, CLAUDIA.
   Claudia.
NOT TRUE,
YOU NEED TWO, GUIDO,
MY CHARMING CASANOVA.
   Guido.
CASANOVA? . . . ME?
   Claudia.
MAYBE EVEN THREE, GUIDO.
   Guido. (*speaks*) Casanova? . . . That's it! What an idea! (*sings*)
ME . . . CASANOVA!
(*He sits and ponders the idea she has just given him.*)
   Claudia. (*seeing he's lost in himself*)
IN A VERY UNUSUAL WAY, ONE TIME I NEEDED YOU.
IN A VERY UNUSUAL WAY, YOU WERE MY FRIEND.
MAYBE IT LASTED A DAY,
MAYBE IT LASTED AN HOUR,
BUT SOMEHOW IT WILL NEVER END.

IN A VERY UNUSUAL WAY, I THINK I'M IN LOVE WITH
   YOU.
IN A VERY UNUSUAL WAY, I WANT TO CRY.
SOMETHING INSIDE ME GOES WEAK,
SOMETHING INSIDE ME SURRENDERS,
AND YOU'RE THE REASON WHY,
YOU'RE THE REASON WHY.

YOU DON'T KNOW WHAT YOU DO TO ME.
YOU DON'T HAVE A CLUE.
YOU CAN'T TELL WHAT IT'S LIKE TO BE ME
LOOKING AT YOU.
IT SCARES ME SO THAT I CAN HARDLY SPEAK.

IN A VERY UNUSUAL WAY, I OWE WHAT I AM TO YOU.
THOUGH AT TIMES IT APPEARS I WON'T STAY,
   I NEVER GO.
SPECIAL TO ME IN MY LIFE,

NINE

SINCE THE FIRST DAY THAT I MET YOU.
HOW COULD I EVER FORGET YOU,
ONCE YOU HAD TOUCHED MY SOUL?

IN A VERY UNUSUAL WAY, YOU'VE MADE ME WHOLE.

Our Lady of the Spa. With the arrival of film star Claudia Nardi, there was no question but that he suddenly seemed stronger.

La Fleur. Contini! The crew arrives tomorrow!

Guido. I am ready!

Our Lady of the Spa. For his cast, he hired everyone at the spa. But I mistrusted his apparent strength. Victories of the kind he needed aren't won so easily.

Guido. Luisa, my angel, light of my life, I am about to enter a realm I have never dared enter before. Wish me luck! (*to himself*) Casanova! What an idea!

Guido.	Claudia.
OH . . .	IN A VERY UNUSUAL WAY
	I OWE WHAT I AM TO YOU
WHAT YOU HAVE DONE FOR ME.	
	THOUGH AT TIMES IT APPEARS I WON'T STAY,
	I NEVER GO.
AS ALWAYS BEFORE, SPECIAL TO ME	
	SPECIAL TO ME IN MY LIFE,
SINCE THAT FIRST DAY.	SINCE THE FIRST DAY THAT I MET YOU.

Guido & Claudia.
HOW COULD I EVER FORGET YOU,
ONCE YOU HAD TOUCHED MY SOUL?

IN A VERY UNUSUAL WAY, YOU'VE MADE ME WHOLE.

(*GUIDO calls in a silk curtain that masks the stage.*)

Guido. (*sings*)
CONTINI SUBMITS
THAT THE FLOPS AREN'T HITS
BECAUSE NO ONE IS WILLING

TO FILM A ROMANTIC SPECTACULAR
THAT'LL USE THE VERNACULAR.

AND HE SAYS FURTHERMORE
THAT THE PRESENT'S A BORE,
BUT HISTORICALLY SPEAKING,
MORE INTERESTING SUBJECTS ARE MYRIAD
IN A PERIOD.
PERIOD!

CONTINI CONTENDS THAT THE PAST
MAKES THE PRESENT LOOK DULL AND HALF-ASSED.
LET OTHER DIRECTORS
INVESTIGATE SECTORS
OF IMAGE AND MEANING
ONCE COMMONLY THOUGHT OF AS CURRENT,
'CAUSE THEY AREN'T – AND WEREN'T.

CONTINI SUGGESTS
THAT TODAY'S NOT THE BEST,
BUT THAT YESTERDAY'S BETTER
AND LONGER AGO IS STILL BETTERER.
ET CETERA, ET CETERA.

AND NOW I HAVE FOUND THE RIGHT LOCATION
THAT PERFECTLY SUITS THIS NEW CREATION,
A PICTURE SO BROAD AND SERPENTINING
THAT IT WILL CONTAIN A WORLD OF MEANING.
AND IT'S ALREADY HERE IN FRONT OF MY NOSE.
THIS IS THE ANSWER TO WHAT I PROPOSE.
VENICE BY DAY – VENICE BY NIGHT,
RIGHT WHERE I AM IS TERRIFIC'LY RIGHT.
(*Speaks*) Everybody on the set for rehearsal with lights!

(*Curtain opens to reveal the SPA PEOPLE as GUIDO's Venetian Company. LUISA sits watching; GUIDO throws her a kiss.*)

 Guido & Spa People.
THIS IS THE GRAND CANAL. (LA LA LA LA LA LA)
ITS RESEMBLANCE TO LIFE IS NOT OBSCURE.
IT IS FILLED WITH THE MILK OF HUMAN KIND-
 NESS

NINE

IN SPITE OF THE FACT IT'S REALLY A SEWER.
BUT DON'T LET THAT SPOIL YOUR MORALE.
IT'S A GRAND CANAL.
  GUIDO.
THIS IS A GONDOLIER.
SEEKING LOVE IS THE CENTER OF HIS LIFE.
BUT HE NEVER WILL GO AS FAR AS WEDLOCK—
THAT WOULD REALLY ANNOY HIS PRESENT WIFE.
HE STRUMS HIS PLAINTIVE PASTORALE.
  ALL.
ON THE GRAND CANAL.

LOOK AT THE PEOPLE IN THE SQUARE,
LOOK AT THE STEEPLE IN THE AIR.
CAN YOU DENY THAT IT'S A STUNNING VIEW?
FACES ARE BRIMMING WITH DELIGHT,
CHILDREN ARE SWIMMING LATE AT NIGHT.
WHY DON'T YOU TRY THAT? IT IS FUN,
AND WHO CAN IT HARM TO FEEL ITS CHARM?

GUIDO & GERMANS.	OTHERS.
I LOVE IT, I LOVE IT,	ROW ME, ROW ME
I LOVE IT I DO	DOWN THE GRAND
ON THE GRAND CANAL.	CANAL,
	ROW ME WITH MY GAL.
I LOVE IT, I LOVE IT,	ROW ME, ROW ME
I'M HAPPY WITH YOU	DOWN THE GRAND
ON THE GRAND CANAL.	CANAL,
	BE MY BOSOM PAL.
ON THE GRAND CANAL.	GRAND CANAL.

  GUIDO.
AND THIS IS A COURTESAN (SHE IS A COURTESAN).
IT'S A SHAME PEOPLE THINK THAT SHE'S A LEECH.
TRUE, SHE ONCE IN A WHILE DESTROYS A MARRIAGE,
BUT OTHER THAN THAT SHE'S REALLY A PEACH,
  ALL.
SWEET AS THE SWEETEST MADRIGAL
ON THE GRAND CANAL.

(*NOTE: An alternate and briefer Grand Canal sequence, which must be used if La Fleur is played by a man, is provided at the back of the script.*)

GUIDO. All right, everybody, get out of the water! (*to the GERMANS*) Frauleins, get your tambourines, get ready for the next scene. (*seeing CLAUDIA in her costume*) Ah, Claudia! Sei bellissima! Il costume e perfetto! (*CLAUDIA and GUIDO argue, dialogue overlapping:*)

CLAUDIA. Davvero? Ma non voglio mettere questo costume! Lo sai perche? Perche questo e il costume che ho meso in "Via Veneto," nel "Giardino dei Terrestri" e nella "Cattedrale dei Sogni." Non me lo metto piu! Ne ho avuto abbastanza di questa parte! (*English Translation:* You think so? Well, I don't want to wear this costume! You know why? Because this is the costume I wore in "Via Veneto,' and in "The Garden of Earthly Delights," and in "Cathedral of Dreams"! I won't wear it anymore! I've had enough of this part!)

GUIDO. (*simultaneously*) Ma che dici? Questo e un costume bellissimo! Fantastico! Incredibile! Sei impazzita? (*English Translation:* What are you talking about? This is a beautiful costume! Fantastic! Incredible! Have you gone crazy?)

CLAUDIA. (*tears off her costume, throwing it on ground*) Guido, you promised me another role! That's why I agreed to stay! I won't play this role anymore! (*She storms off.*)

GUIDO. (*calling off*) All right, all right! I'll give you a different role! You can play . . . (*Seeing LUISA, an idea strikes.*) . . . you can play Beatrice, Casanova's wife. It's a wonderful role, very challenging.

CLAUDIA. (*re-enters*) Va bene! (*She exits.*)

GUIDO. (*in mocking imitation*) Va bene! (*picks up costume*) Five million lire! (*SPA PEOPLE pass, rehearsing a number. LA FLEUR is with them.*)

LA FLEUR. Contini, you're a genius.

GUIDO. (*another idea*) That's because you are such an inspiration, Madame La Fleur. Why don't you try on this costume . . . Perfect! You're in the film! (*LA FLEUR exits. GUIDO runs to kiss LUISA, then returns to the GERMANS, who are entering with tambourines. NECROPHORUS enters and watches. To GERMANS:*) Frauleins, grazie. This is a very sexy Italian dance. It is called the tarantella . . .

GERMANS. Tar-an-tella . . .

GUIDO. . . . Yes. And it's in celebration of the bite of the Devil. Watch carefully. (*GUIDO performs SARRAGHINA's tambourine routine.*) You do it! (*GERMANS give it a try; not too good.*)

GUIDO. (*to audience*) Numerous rehearsals later. (*SPA PEOPLE rush on and join the GERMANS in the SARRAGHINA*

NINE

tambourine routine. Suddenly CARLA enters with divorce papers, wending her way through the rehearsal, ending up near LUISA. GUIDO sees her and pulls her away from LUISA. Snatches of their argument are heard over the music and dancing.) What the hell are you doing here? Why are you talking to my wife?

CARLA. Guido, my divorce! It's final!

GUIDO. Divorce? I said nothing about a divorce! I'm not leaving my wife! Are you crazy? Now get out of here! (*GUIDO throws down the divorce papers and goes back to the rehearsal. CARLA is in shock. She slowly picks up the papers as—)*

GUIDO & SOME.	OTHERS.
THIS IS THE GRAND CANAL.	ROW ME, ROW ME DOWN THE GRAND CANAL.
ITS RESEMBLANCE TO LIFE IS NOT OBSCURE.	
IT IS FILLED WITH THE MILK OF HUMAN KINDNESS IN SPITE OF THE FACT IT'S REALLY A SEWER.	ROW ME WITH MY GAL. ROW ME, ROW ME DOWN THE GRAND CANAL.
	BE MY BOSOM PAL.

ALL.
BUT DON'T LET THAT SPOIL YOUR MORALE.
IT'S A GRAND CANAL.

GUIDO. Everybody, change your costumes for the boudoir rehearsal! (*He and the others exit. CARLA, stunned and humiliated, tries to smoothe her crumpled divorce papers. SPA LADY enters in boudoir costume.)*

OUR LADY OF THE SPA. (*sings*)
EVERY GIRL IN VENICE IS IN LOVE WITH CASANOVA.
EVERY GIRL HAS KISSED HIM ONCE OR TWICE.
EVERY GIRL IN VENICE IS IN LOVE WITH CASANOVA.
AS LONG AS CASANOVA PAYS HER PRICE.

EVERY GIRL IN VENICE IS EXPECTING CASANOVA.
EVERY GIRL IS COMBING OUT HER HAIR.
(*Other SPA LADIES begin joining her, as they enter in their boudoir costumes.)*
COUNTING EVERY MINUTE TILL THEY SEE THEIR CASANOVA

AND STARING OUT THEIR WINDOWS EVERYWHERE.
EVERY GIRL IN VENICE WANTS TO HEAR FROM CASANOVA.
SHE WILL BE THE ONLY GIRL FOR HIM.
EVERY GIRL IS GRINNING EAR TO EAR FOR CASANOVA
AND WAITING TO ATTEND HIS EVERY WHIM . . .

(*LITTLE BOYS enter as pages, flanking LA FLEUR, dressed in CLAUDIA's abandoned costume, MAMA MADDELENA, and CLAUDIA. GUIDO enters.*)

    Guido — Casanova. (*sings*)
I, CASANOVA, HAVE COME TO VENICE
(*indicating CLAUDIA*)
WITH MY DEAR WIFE, BEATRICE, MI AMORE,
HERE TO TAKE A REST, ENJOY THE WATERS AND THE FOOD,
AND BE WITH HER, THE APPLE OF MY CUORE.
    Mama Maddelena. (*as "CARLA"—MARIA*)
CASANOVA!
    Guido — Casanova.
MARIA! WHAT ARE YOU DOING HERE?
    Maddelena — Maria.
I'M STAYING AT THE HOSTELERIA CALDISSIMA, NUMERO VENTI VENTI.
DROP BY TONIGHT AT TEN O'CLOCK, I'LL GIVE YOU PLENTY.
    Guido — Casanova.
I CAN'T BELIEVE HOW MY GOOD FORTUNE STILL DOES SERVE ME.
SO MUCH ROMANCE AT HAND, I REALLY DON'T DESERVE ME.

(*GUIDO sings with BOUDOIR LADIES.*)
AMOR, I LOVE THEM ALL, EVERY BEAUTY,
SHORT OR TALL, THERE'S A DUTY
TO MAKE LOVE TO EACH AND ALL.
AMOR, IT'S MY PROFOUND OBLIGATION
TO GO ROUND EVERY NATION
AND MAKE LOVE TO ONE AND ALL.
YES, I HAVE LIVED AND BREATHED AND SLEPT AMOR.
I FREELY GIVE AND DO ACCEPT AMOR.

NINE

BIG AMOR, SMALL AMOR, ALL MY LIFE HAS BEEN AMOR.
I'VE ALWAYS KNOWN WHAT I AM LIVING FOR—AMOR!

GUIDO—CASANOVA.
BUT ALAS, I AM DISTRESSED BY ALL THIS BEAUTY FINE
IF I MUST CHOOSE BUT ONE CONCUBINE.

(*LADIES scream "Me! Me!"*)

GUIDO. Get ready for the next set-up! (*ALL leave to change for next scene. NECROPHORUS steps forward.*)

NECROPHORUS.
CONTINI CAN'T SERIOUSLY BELIEVE WE WILL ACCEPT THIS FATUOUS RENDERING OF A SEVENTEENTH CENTURY OPERA AS AN EXCUSE FOR A MOVIE.
NO WAY, NO WAY, NO WAY!

GUIDO'S MOTHER. (*entering*)
IF ONLY GUIDO HAD BECOME A PRIEST OR A LAWYER,
BUT NO, HE MAKES THESE FILMS I CAN'T EXPLAIN TO MY FRIENDS.

(*NECROPHORUS and GUIDO's MOTHER step aside, away from the action.*)

GUIDO. (*running into place for scene with CLAUDIA, MADDELENA, and LA FLEUR*) Places, places! (*BOUDOIR NUNS enter. GUIDO "shoots himself" as if with a gun, collapses.*)

CLAUDIA—BEATRICE.
CASANOVA, YOU MUST RELAX.
YOU WILL EXHAUST YOURSELF AND SOON BECOME TOO STANCO.
LOOK, I HAVE PREPARED A PICNIC BASKET, PROSCIUTTO, OLIVES,
AND OF COURSE YOUR FAVORITE, VINO—BIANCO.

(*LUISA stares in horror.*)

GUIDO—CASANOVA.
BEATRICE . . . BEATRICE . . .
ONLY YOU WILL I EVER SEE,
FOREVER WILL YOU BE MY TRUE LOVE.
I'LL FORSWEAR ALL OTHERS FOR THEE,
NO, NEVER WILL I HAVE A NEW LOVE.
NO NEW LOVE, NO NEW LOVE,
AND YOU WILL BE MY TRUE LOVE.

Guido–Casanova & Claudia–Beatrice.
NO NEW LOVE, NO NEW LOVE,
AND YOU WILL BE MY TRUE LOVE.
　Boudoir Nuns.
CASANOVA TAKES A VOW,
TELLING BEATRICE NOW
THERE WILL NEVER BE ANOTHER WOMAN IN HIS
　LIFE BUT HER,
NOW UNTIL FOREVERMORE.
　Maddelena–Maria. (*repeating CARLA's "Vatican" moves*) Casanova, I'm still waiting for you!
　Guido–Casanova. Maria!
　Boudoir Nuns.
EVERMORE.
　Maddelena–Maria. Cootchie-coo . . . !
　Guido–Casanova. (*to MARIA*)
ONLY YOU CAN STIR IN MY BREAST
THE FIRE OF AN ENDLESS PASSION.
LATE TONIGHT I'LL BE IN YOUR BED.
EXPECT ME IN THE USUAL FASHION.
OUR FASHION, OUR FASHION,
AH, FIRE OF AN ENDLESS PASSION.
　Guido–Casanova & Maddelena–Maria.
OUR FASHION, OUR FASHION,
AH, FIRE OF AN ENDLESS PASSION.
(*They proceed to make love in a farce of GUIDO–CARLA acrobatics, ending in wrist-wrestling on the floor.*)
　Boudoir Nuns.
CASANOVA BREAKS A VOW.
WHERE IS BEATRICE NOW?
THERE WAS NOT TO BE ANOTHER WOMAN IN HIS LIFE
　BUT HER,
NOW UNTIL FOREVERMORE, EVERMORE.
(*They exit.*)
　La Fleur. Casanova!
　Guido–Casanova. Claudietta! (*He goes to her. CLAUDIA, hearing her name, turns to watch. Note that LUISA and CARLA have observed the last "scene", a mockery of their relationship with GUIDO.*)
ONLY YOU BRING OUT FROM MY SOUL
THE POETRY THAT I HAVE WRITTEN.
NOT ONE LINE WOULD I HAVE COMPOSED
IF I HAD NOT BY YOU BEEN SMITTEN.

NINE

CLAUDIA. (*angry at seeing the farce*) Guido . . . !
LUISA. (*totally humiliated, has seen enough, sings*)
GUIDO . . . NO . . . !
(*CLAUDIA, MADDELENA, and LA FLEUR exit. GUIDO and LUISA fight over harsh tarantella music.*)
GUIDO. Luisa, ma che cosa?
LUISA. Come hai potuto fare una cosa cosi?
GUIDO. Che cosa? Che dici?
LUISA. You've made a joke of my love!
GUIDO. Ah, Luisa, tu drammatizzi troppo!
LUISA. Guido, mi sento ridicola! Davanti a tutti!
GUIDO. Luisa, it's only a farce!
LUISA. *My life is not a farce!*

(*SPA PEOPLE begin to enter for the film's finale.*)

GUIDO. (*trying to quiet her*) Luisa, it is only a film. Capisci? Solo un film.
LUISA. Ah—solo un film . . . La mia vita, solo un film? Il nostro amore, solo un film?
GUIDO. Luisa, you're taking this too seriously.
LUISA. Ma hai *tradito* il nostro amore!
GUIDO. Va bene! You feel betrayed? I'll cut the scene from the film!
LUISA. (*hand on heart*) But not from *here!*
GUIDO. Luisa, listen to me! As an artist I have to use everything in my life! Everything!
LUISA. Fine! Use it! But use it well! (*She runs from him.*)
GUIDO. Luisa!
LUISA. No, no more!
GUIDO. *Luisa!*
LUISA. Basta! Va' a lavoro. Va' all'inferno. Go to hell!

(*GUIDO, about to rush after her, cannot because the finale is beginning and he must join in. LUISA sobs in a corner. CARLA stares aghast from another corner. GUIDO tries to act as if all is well.*)

GUIDO & SPA PEOPLE.

THIS IS THE	THIS IS THE	ROW ME,
GRAND CANAL,	GRAND CANAL.	ROW ME,
THIS IS THE	I LOVE IT,	ROW ME,
GRAND CANAL,	I LOVE IT,	ROW ME,

IT'S RESEM-
  BLANCE TO
  LIFE
IS NOT OBSCURE.
	I LOVE IT I DO
	  ON THE GRAND
	  CANAL.
		DOWN THE
		  GRAND
		  CANAL.

IT IS FILLED
  WITH THE
  MILK
  OF HUMAN
  KINDNESS
IN SPITE OF THE
  FACT
IT'S REALLY A
  SEWER.
	I LOVE IT,
	  I LOVE IT,
	I'M HAPPY WITH
	  YOU
	ON THE GRAND
	  CANAL,
		ROW ME WITH
		  MY GAL.
		ROW ME,
		  ROW ME,
		DOWN THE
		  GRAND
		  CANAL,
		BE MY BOSOM
		  PAL.

BUT DON'T LET THAT SPOIL YOUR MORALE.
IT'S STILL A GRAND
CANAL . . . !
  GUIDO. Cut! Print!

(*Exit ALL except GUIDO, OUR LADY OF THE SPA, LUISA, and CARLA.*)

  OUR LADY OF THE SPA. As far as I could see, his creative life had become, by now, so closely bound to his personal that once his personal life began to fall apart, his creative had to fall apart as well; there was just no separation anymore.
  GUIDO. Luisa?
  OUR LADY OF THE SPA. La sua signora non e qui.
  GUIDO. Claudia?
  OUR LADY OF THE SPA. La Signorina Nardi non e qui.
  GUIDO. Carla?
  OUR LADY OF THE SPA. She's at the station. (*She exits.*)
  GUIDO. Carla, listen, there's been a misunderstanding here!
  CARLA. I agree.
  GUIDO. No-no, listen, that isn't what I mean! Look, I love you very much! Why complicate this love? What's between you and me is so simple!
  CARLA. Sure, Guido. Simple. (*sings*)
SIMPLE THESE AFFAIRS THAT TOUCH THE HEART.
SIMPLE ARE THE WAYS OF LOVE.
SIMPLE AS THE TOUCH OF ANOTHER'S HAND.
SIMPLE ENOUGH FOR ANYONE TO UNDERSTAND
BUT YOU . . .

NINE

Guido. Carla! Carlissima!
Carla.
SIMPLE ARE THE WAYS WE COME APART.
SIMPLE AS A BABE IS NEW.
SIMPLE AS A TREE, AND AS SIMPLE AS A CLOUD,
IT'S AS SIMPLE AS THE SIMPLEST THINGS HAVE
  ALWAYS BEEN.
SIMPLE AS THE SUN AND THE MOON AND THE STARS
  IN THE SKY,
SIMPLE ARE THE WAYS WE SAY GOODBYE.
  Claudia. (*entering*) I live in Paris with a man named Michel Boulon . . .
  Carla.
SIMPLE THESE AFFAIRS THAT TOUCH THE HEART . . .
  Claudia. Michel is fifty-three. He's an investment banker, very handsome, charming, wealthy. The house we live in overlooks Parc Monceau.
  Carla.
. . . SIMPLE ARE THE WAYS OF LOVE . . .
  Claudia. When I'm not making a film, I get up around seven-thirty, have breakfast with Michel, then walk, if the weather's good, to the Studio Waker in Place Clichy, where I take a dance class. For lunch, I generally eat in a small bar in the basement of the school. After lunch I take an acting class.
  Carla.
. . . SIMPLE AS A TREE . . .
  Claudia. Acting is what I care about, Guido. And Michel understands. Michel does not distract me. I've made choices in my life. I know what I want.
  Carla.
. . . SIMPLE ARE THE WAYS WE SAY GOODBYE.
  Claudia. Ciao, Guido. (*CLAUDIA exits.*)
  Carla. Ciao. (*CARLA exits.*)
  Guido. Luisa!
  Luisa. (*sings*)
BE ON YOUR OWN.
YOU'VE ALWAYS TALKED ABOUT YOUR NEED TO
  TRAVEL,
NOW GO OFF, UNRAVEL ON YOUR OWN.
GO FIND SOME RESTAURANT ATTENDANT,
GO SHOW HER HOW INDEPENDENT YOU HAVE
  GROWN.
GO ON . . .

BE ON YOUR WAY.
THERE'S NOT A SINGLE REASON I CAN FIND
TO MAKE ME WANT TO KEEP YOU ONE MORE DAY.
THERE ISN'T ANY SORT OF WORD THAT YOU COULD SAY.
THERE ISN'T ANY SORT OF PRICE THAT YOU COULD PAY.
THERE ISN'T ANY SORT OF MAGIC
TO AVOID THIS TRAGI-COMIC LITTLE PLAY
WE NEED TO PLAY—
BE ON YOUR WAY.
GO ON. . .

NO NEED TO CARRY OUT THIS MASQUERADE
WHEN ALL THAT WE'RE ABOUT'S BEGUN TO FADE.

I SET YOU FREE.
THERE'S NOT MUCH LONGER TO COMPLAIN,
I'LL SOON RELIEVE YOU OF YOUR PAIN
WHEN I SET YOU FREE.
IF THAT IS ALL YOU WISH TO HAVE, THEN I AGREE.
NO NEED FOR THANKS, YOUR JUST REWARDS WILL BE MY FEE.
GO OFF AND LIVE YOUR PETTY FICTIONS
FULL OF BLATANT CONTRADICTIONS YOU CAN'T SEE,
AND WHAT WILL BE
IS THAT YOU'LL LEAVE,
AND YOU'LL TAKE WITH YOU ALL YOU OWN FROM A TO Z
. . . AND ALL OF ME.

(*LUISA exits through the audience. For the first time in the show, GUIDO is alone on stage.*)

GUIDO.
NOT SINCE CHARLIE CHAPLIN
HAS THERE EVER BEEN A FILM DIRECTOR LIKE THIS,
GUIDO CONTINI.

EVERYTHING HE DOES GETS WORLD ATTENTION
WHETHER IT'S A HIT OR A MISS,
GUIDO CONTINI.

HE WRITES THE SCRIPT . . .

NINE

I CAN'T MAKE THIS MOVIE, THERE'S NO WAY THAT
  I'LL COMPLETE IT.
I CAN'T BEAR TO SEE THE CAMERAS ROLL.
PROBLEM IS THE SUBJECT, THERE'S NO PLEASANT
  WAY TO TREAT IT.
PROBLEM IS THE AUTHOR'S LOST CONTROL.
HOW I WISH IT DIDN'T HAVE TO BE SO,
BUT WE CUT THE LOSSES STARTING NOW.
STRIKE THE SET AND KEEP IT FOR SOME SIDE SHOW.
TELL THE CAST AND CREW THAT THEY CAN ALL GO.

FIND ANOTHER GENIUS, I CAN'T BE ONE OR BECOME
  ONE.
I CAN'T EVEN TELL HOW I'D BEGIN.
HELP LUISA, HELP ME, HELP ME MAMA, HELP ME
  SOMEONE.
HERE'S A PLACE WHERE I HAVE NEVER BEEN.
GUIDO OUT IN SPACE WITH NO DIRECTION,
GUIDO AT A LOSS FOR WHAT TO SAY,
GUIDO WITH NO INTERVENING ACTORS,
GUIDO AT THE MERCY OF DETRACTORS,
GUIDO HERE WITH NO ONE ELSE BUT GUIDO
THIS DAY!

(*He slumps in despair. Enter LA FLEUR, NECROPHORUS, and LINA/LEO. They cross behind the desolate GUIDO, who fantasizes:*)

NECROPHORUS. All in all, I think what's happened is for the best. Certainly, if he hadn't shot himself, the critics would have shot him down. No, this film was a disaster—superficial, salacious, self-serving, self-indulgent . . . I'm amazed he had the perception to see all that. Good thing you insured his life! (*Exeunt, LINA/LEO leaving a pistol near GUIDO before going.*)
  GUIDO. Is this part of my film, or isn't it?

(*Enter GUIDO's MOTHER.*)

GUIDO'S MOTHER. Guido!
  GUIDO. Mama! . . . Oh Mama, am I glad to see you! You've no idea how much you've been on my mind!
  GUIDO'S MOTHER. And you on mine. Guido, listen, darling, bad news: you're going to die. (*GUIDO keels over.*) Guido, get

up. I didn't say you were going to die right away.

GUIDO. (*sitting up*) You didn't?

GUIDO'S MOTHER. No . . . Of course, that doesn't mean I know *when* your death's been planned.

GUIDO. It's been *planned?*

GUIDO'S MOTHER. Oh, everything's planned up here. Planned very carefully.

GUIDO. Listen, does this plan, by any chance, have something to do with how one's films are doing?

GUIDO'S MOTHER. No, I don't think so . . . Though frankly, from what I've seen of this film you've been working on, death might be the best way out.

GUIDO. Mama! How can you say a thing like that?

GUIDO'S MOTHER. I hope you don't have any of your own money in it.

GUIDO. Mama, are you joking?

GUIDO'S MOTHER. No, the film is terrible, and you're going to die. I don't believe the two are related.

GUIDO. If the film was good, would I live?

GUIDO'S MOTHER. Really, I don't think it has anything to do with that. Your death is your death. I saw it in the books . . . in the "Inevitable Column."

GUIDO. I'm told they occasionally revise that.

GUIDO'S MOTHER. Oh no, I don't think so.

GUIDO. (*furious*) Why didn't you warn me about this when I was young?

GUIDO'S MOTHER. I didn't want to spoil your childhood.

GUIDO. Now you're spoiling my old age!

GUIDO'S MOTHER. You're not old yet. Pray God you get there. Anyway, that's the news from up above. Shape up! (*She exits.*)

GUIDO. Mama, wait! Wait! What's it like up there? Mama, what's it like? . . . I wish she hadn't come. (*He ponders.*) It's certainly not a *bad* idea for a film: the last days of a director's once brilliant career. Takes place in a spa . . . And at the end . . . (*He sees the pistol; picks up the pistol, puts it to his temple, and then collapses onto his back. Enter LITTLE GUIDO.*)

LITTLE GUIDO. (*sings*)
GUIDO . . . GUIDO . . .
(*GUIDO rises, looks disgustedly at the ineffective pistol.*)
SCRAPING KNEES, TYING SHOES,
STARTING SCHOOL, PAYING DUES,
FINDING THERE'S NO WAY

NINE

WE CAN SPEND A LIFETIME PLAYING BALL—
PART OF GETTING TALL.

(*LITTLE GUIDO approaches the forlorn figure of GUIDO.*)

LEARNING MORE, KNOWING LESS,
SIMPLE WORDS, TENDERNESS—
PART OF GETTING TALL.

(*He sits with GUIDO.*)

GUIDO, YOU'RE NOT CRAZY, YOU'RE ALL RIGHT.
EVERYONE WANTS EVERYONE IN SIGHT . . .
BUT KNOWING YOU HAVE NO ONE IF YOU TRY TO
   HAVE THEM ALL
IS PART OF TYING SHOES,
PART OF STARTING SCHOOL,
PART OF SCRAPING KNEES IF WE SHOULD FALL—
PART OF GETTING TALL.

(*LITTLE GUIDO pushes GUIDO to his feet, gives GUIDO his baton. GUIDO looks to the front, as the PEOPLE in his mind—the GERMANS, the ITALIANS, OUR LADY OF THE SPA, NECROPHORUS, LA FLEUR, GUIDO'S MOTHER, CLAUDIA, CARLA, the NUN—enter in turn. When they are assembled in their original places, he prepares to "conduct his orchestra" . . . but sees one empty place . . . LUISA's.*)

  GUIDO. (*sings*)
GUIDO CONTINI, LUSIA DEL FORNO,
ACTRESS WITH DREAMS AND A LIFE OF HER OWN,
PASSIONATE, WILD, AND IN LOVE IN LIVORNO,
SINGING TOGETHER ALL NIGHT ON THE PHONE . . .
  LUISA. (*appearing in the distance*)
LONG AGO . . .
  GUIDO. (*He does not see her.*)
SOMEONE ELSE AGO,
HOW I NEED YOU SO,
AND I'VE BEEN THE LAST TO KNOW IT . . .
(*He beckons to LITTLE GUIDO.*)
GUIDO . . . CARO MIO . . .

TIME TO GO OFF ON MY OWN.
YOU BELONG IN YOUR MOTHER'S ARMS.
EACH OF US IN OUR PLACE, WE'LL BE FINE.
I'LL BE FORTY AND YOU'LL BE . . .
   Little Guido.
YOU'LL BE FORTY AND I'LL BE . . .
   Guido & Little Guido.
. . . NINE.

(*GUIDO gives the baton to LITTLE GUIDO and watches the BOY "conduct his orchestra" in a wordless and nostalgic reprise of "Be Italian." As LITTLE GUIDO conducts, GUIDO sees LUISA in the distance and runs to embrace her. And the curtain falls.*)

ALTERNATE GRAND CANAL SEQUENCE

(*Continuing from page 54.*)

... SWEET AS THE SWEETEST MADRIGAL
ON THE GRAND CANAL.

Guido. Frauleins, sing for me. (*ALL exit except GUIDO, LUISA, and GERMAN WOMEN.*)

German Women.
EVERY GIRL IN VENICE IS IN LOVE VIT CASANOVA.
EVERY GIRL HAS KISSED HIM VUNCE OR TVICE.
EVERY GIRL IN VENICE IS IN LOVE VIT CASANOVA
AS LONG AS CASANOVA PAYS HER PRICE.

Guido. Wunderbar, Frauleins. Get your tambourines. (*GERMAN (MEN and) WOMEN grab tambourines, group around GUIDO.*) This is called the tarantella ...

Germans. Tar-an-tella ...

Guido. ... Yes. It is a sexy Italian dance, done in celebration of the bite of the Devil. Watch carefully. (*GUIDO performs SARRAGHINA's tambourine dance.*) You do it! (*GERMANS give it a try; not too good.*) Maybe it looks better from out front.

(*GUIDO goes into the audience as the GERMANS bang their tambourines again. Suddenly CLAUDIA enters screaming over the MUSIC, waving a script.*)

Claudia. Guido! GUIDO, I QUIT!

Guido. (*silencing the GERMANS and the orchestra*) Stop. STOP! ... Claudia, what's wrong?

Claudia. Guido, I stayed because you promised me a different role. (*sings*)
THIS IS THE PART I'VE BEEN PLAYING FOREVER.
NOTHING HAS CHANGED AND YOU PROMISED IT
  WOULD.
GUIDO CONTINI, WATCH CLAUDIA NARDI
LEAVING THE SET OF THIS MOVIE FOR GOOD.

Guido. Claudia, I need you.

(*CARLA enters waving at GUIDO, holding her divorce papers.*)

Carla. Yoo-hoo!

Guido. Carla. Oh my God. (*to the audience*) Somebody wave to her.

CARLA. GUIDO!
GUIDO. (*to the audience*) Too late. Anybody named Guido, wave to her.
CARLA. (*approaching GUIDO*) Guido, I got my divorce!
GUIDO. (*to CARLA*) Divorce?!
CARLA. Now we can be married!
GUIDO. Married?! (*sings*)
HOW CAN THAT BE WHEN I'M ALREADY MARRIED?
WHAT HAVE I SAID THAT COULD MAKE YOU BELIEVE THAT?
CARLA. But, Guido . . . (*sings*)
THIS IS THE PAPER I'VE WAITED AND WORKED FOR,
LIVING ON HOPE AND BELIEVING IN YOU.
GUIDO CONTINI AND CARLA ALBANESE . . .
GUIDO. (*quietly*)
WE CAN STILL BE TOGETHER . . .
CARLA.
TUTTO CAPITO.
GUIDO. Carla . . .
CARLA.
TUTTO FINITO!
GUIDO. Carla . . .
LUISA. (*rising*) Guido, you told me that this was all over with.
GUIDO. Luisa!
LUISA. (*sings*)
GUIDO CONTINI, LUISI CONTINI:
COMING TO VENICE AND HAVING A BALL—
GETTING AWAY FROM IT ALL—
LUISA, CARLA, & CLAUDIA.
LIAR!!!
GUIDO. Stop! (*MUSIC stops.*) This is not what I want.

(*A bell tone, a lighting change, and at once we are seeing an alternate world that exists only in GUIDO's imagination: LUISA and CARLA hug like old friends, CLAUDIA assumes a "goddess" pose. All the WOMEN sing.*)

LUISA, CARLA, CLAUDIA, & GERMAN WOMEN.
EVERY GIRL IN VENICE IS IN LOVE WITH CASANOVA.
GUIDO. This is what I want!
LUISA, CARLA, CLAUDIA, & GERMAN WOMEN.
EVERY GIRL HAS KISSED HIM ONCE OR TWICE.

NINE

GUIDO. Why can't life be like this?

(*A harsh chord, and we jolt back to reality.*)

CLAUDIA. I'm leaving.
GUIDO. Claudia! (*She exits.*)
CARLA. Don't try to call me.
GUIDO. Carla! (*She walks away.*)
LUISA. This was your last chance.
GUIDO. Luisa! (*She walks away.*)
LA FLEUR. (*entering, followed by several SPA PEOPLE dressed for the finale of the film*) Contini! This is costing me a fortune! We are falling behind! Proceed!

(*More SPA PEOPLE enter. GUIDO, about to rush after LUISA, cannot because the finale is beginning and he must join in . . .*)

(*Rejoining the original script on page 60.*)

PROP LIST

PRE-SET ON STAGE:
A baton (on GUIDO's podium)
A gondola pole (by GONDOLIER's box)
A gun (inside LINA's/LEO's box)
A towel to wrap around LITTLE GUIDO (inside GUIDO's podium)
Four tambourines for BOYS

OFF RIGHT:

LITTLE GUIDO:
Gift box with boa inside

OFF LEFT:

GUIDO's MOTHER:
A black parasol (Act I)
A white parasol (Act II)
LITTLE GUIDO:
A pair of cymbals
GERMANS:
Five tambourines (one for GUIDO)
ITALIANS:
Seven tambourines
CARLA:
Divorce papers
LINA/LEO:
A gun

IN ORCHESTRA PIT:
A tambourine

COSTUME PLOT

In the original Broadway production of NINE (designed by William Ivey Long), the women were dressed in a wide range of fashion styles. While the costumes were set in no particular period, they were always meant to be glamorous and flattering to the performers, and adhered to a consistent color scheme.

In all of Act I (and the opening of Act II) the entire cast was dressed in *black*.

When Guido began to shoot his film (the Grand Canal sequence), the stage suddenly filled with color:

Grand Canal Opening: all the women were in *green*
"Every Girl in Venice"/"Amor": predominantly *pink*
Grand Canal Finale: *red*

Finally, for the last scene of the show, the women returned in *all-white* versions of their Act I costumes.

Only Guido, Luisa, and Little Guido remained in *black* throughout the show.

GUIDO CONTINI

Black shirt
Black slacks
Black shoes
Black silk scarf

Casanova:
Black cape

GUIDO AT AN EARLY AGE (YOUNG GUIDO)

Act I
Black dress shirt
Black scarf (attached to shirt)
Black shorts
Nude undershorts
Black ankle socks
Black sandals
White linen towel (props)
Black knee pads

Act II
Grand Canal
Green I:
   Repeat shirt, shorts, socks, sandals

Casanova:
   Green beaded jacket
   Green satin "knickers"
   Green milliskin tights
   Green turban w/feathers
   Green ballet slippers w/bead trim
   Black full-face mask

Finale:
   Repeat black shirt, scarf, shorts, socks, sandals

LUISA

Act I
Black velvet jacket w/black jet trim
Black silk brocade blouse
Black skirt
Black leather pumps w/suede inserts
Black opaque ntw pantyhose

Black briefs
Wedding band & engagement ring
Gold locket & chain

Act II
Repeat above

CARLA

Act I
Black lace unitard w/velvet belt
Black open-toe high heel sandals
"Lucky Strike" ntw support pantyhose nude
Black nun's habit
Black nun's headdress

Act II
Opening:
  Repeat above
Grand Canal
Green I:
  Repeat body suit, shoes
  Add: Black taffeta jacket w/ruffled collar

Finale:
  White beaded body suit w/silver belt, white high-heel
    open-toe sandals

CLAUDIA

Act I
Black unitard
Black sweater
Black T-strap shoes
Gold cross on gold chain
Gold ankle bracelet
Gold ring w/black heart
Diamond stud earrings

Act II
Opening:
  Repeat above

Grand Canal
Green II:
  White-to-green one shoulder "goddess" gown

White corset
　　White sleeve
　　White pumps
　　Hanes Alive ntw pantyhose barely there
　　Beige briefs
　　Rhinestone earrings w/green stone

Casanova: (Beatrice):

Red beaded bodice
Green brocade beaded pannier
Green brocade shoes
Repeat rhinestone earrings
Dark brown Marie Antoinette wig w/red trim

Finale:
　　White "goddess" gown
　　Repeat white shoes
　　Rhinestone dangle earrings

GUIDO'S MOTHER

Act I
Black sheer print overdress
Black satin slip
Black horsehair hat
Black semi-sheer pantyhose
Black briefs
Black med. heel pumps w/strap
Grey pearl necklace & earrings
Black parasol (props)

Act II
Repeat above
Add black acrobatic shoes

Finale:
　　White sheer print overdress
　　White satin slip
　　White opaque ntw pantyhose
　　White horsehair hat
　　White med. heel shoes w/strap
　　White parasol (props)

NINE

LILIANE LA FLEUR

Act I
Black chiffon skirt
Black beaded jacket w/fur collar
Black fur hat
Sheer energy ntw pantyhose nude
Capezio H & S black ntw pantyhose
Black satin pumps
Rhinestone earrings
Black feather boa (props)

Act II
Opening:
  Repeat above
Grand Canal

Casanova: (Claudietta):
  White-to-green one-piece "goddess" gown
  White satin pumps
  Rhinestone earrings w/green stone

Finale:
  White chiffon skirt
  White beaded jacket w/fur collar
  White fur hat
  White opaque ntw pantyhose
  White pumps
  Rhinestone earrings

LINA DARLING

Act I
Black unitard
Black snakeskin pumps
Black trenchcoat
Black jacket
Capezio H & S ntw pantyhose suntan
Black sunglasses (props)
Long fake fingernail
Black lace mantilla

Act II
Opening:
  Repeat above

Grand Canal
Green I:
  Repeat unitard, jacket, heels, glasses
  Add: Black hood, green velvet tricorn w/mask

Green II:
  Repeat unitard, jacket, heels, glasses
  Add: Green brocade hat w/feathers

Casanova:
  Sparkle tights
  Pink teddy & corset
  Pink mob cap w/pink ringlets
  Mules
  Repeat sunglasses

Red Coperto:
  Red cape
  Red hat
  Red gloves
  Red sparkle shoes
  Red sunglasses

Finale:
  Silver unitard
  White open toe pumps
  White trenchcoat
  White sunglasses

STEPHANIE NECROPHORUS

Act I
Black 2-piece suit
Black straw picture hat
Black furs
Black pumps
Black gloves
L'eggs sheer energy ntw pantyhose nude
Black opaque ntw pantyhose
Black w/gold earrings
Black lace mantilla
Black briefs

Act II
Opening:
  Repeat above

Finale:
    White 2-piece suit
    White straw picture hat
    White furs
    White pumps
    White opaque ntw pantyhose
    White briefs

OUR LADY OF THE SPA

Act I
Black kimono
Black headband
Black bodystocking
Capezio H & S ntw pantyhose, suntan
Black opaque ntw pantyhose
Black sandals w/tie ankle straps
1 black earring
Black fan (props)
Black lace mantilla

Act II
Opening:
    Repeat above
    Add white mask w/feathers (props)
Grand Canal

Green I:
    Green beaded "gondolier" unitard
    Green velvet tricorn w/mask
    Green brocade shoes
    Repeat black headband

Casanova:
    Pink teddy & corset
    Sparkle tights
    Red brocade shoes
    Repeat black headband
    White fan (props)
    Pink ribbon neckband w/pendant

Red Coperto:
    Repeat sparkle tights
    Repeat black headband

Repeat red brocade shoes
  Red feather pannier
  Nude net leotard w/feather & bead trim
  Repeat mask w/feathers (props)
  (No white wig)

Finale:
  White kimono
  White headband
  White sandals w/tie ankle straps
  White opaque ntw pantyhose
  1 white pearl earring

MAMA MADDALENA

Act I
Black gown w/ruffled side "fin"
Black jacket w/black jet "star" trim
Black "lacy" spike-heel pumps
Beige ntw pantyhose
Black opaque ntw pantyhose
Black jet teardrop earrings
Black bracelets
Rings
Black lace mantilla

Act II

Opening:
  Repeat above
Grand Canal
Green I:
  Repeat black gown, shoes
  Add: Sparkle tights, green gloves, black turban, green velvet tricorn (no mask)

Green II:
  Repeat sparkle tights
  Beige gown w/side fin & green sequins
  White organdy "shell" hat
  Beige spike-heel pumps

Casanova: (Maria):
  Green lace bodice w/green brocade skirt

NINE

   Maroon covered pannier fram
   Maroon milliskin tights

SARRAGHINA

Act I
Black nuns habit
Black nuns headdress
Black men's character shoes
Black lace-trimmed corset
Black lace knee-length pants
Gold hoop earrings
Black lace mantilla

Act II
Opening:
   Repeat corset, pants, mantilla
Grand Canal

Green I:
   Green cape
   Green gloves
   Black hood
   Green velvet tricorn w/mask
   Green sparkle shoes

Red Coperto:
   Red cape
   Red hat
   Red gloves
   Red sparkle shoes

Finale:
   White nun's habit
   White nun's headdress
   White men's character shoes

MARIA

Act I
Black "pouff" dress
Black lace jacket w/scattered sequin accents
Black w/pewter high-heel, open-toe sandals
Hanes Alive ntw pantyhose barely there
Capezio H & S ntw black pantyhose

Black textured daisy pattern pantyhose
Black briefs
Rhinestone & jet drop earrings
Crystal & jet bracelet
Black lace mantilla

Act II
Opening:
  Repeat above
Grand Canal

Green I:
  Repeat black dress
  Add: Sparkle tights, green gloves, green brocade shoes, black hood, green velvet tricorn (no mask)

Green II:
  Repeat dress, shoes, sparkle tights
  Add: Green brocade hat w/feathers

Casanova I:
  Repeat sparkle tights
  Pink teddy & corset
  Pink mob cap w/pink ringlets
  Mules

Casanova II:
  Repeat teddy, corset, tights
  Add: Black "flying nuns" hat, red brocade shoes

Finale:
  White "pouff" dress
  White w/pewter high-heel, open-toe sandals
  White opaque ntw pantyhose
  White briefs
  Rhinestone drop earrings
  Crystal bracelet

A VENETIAN GONDOLIER

Act I
Black "shawl" skirt
Black T-shirt
Black sandals
Capezio H & S ntw pantyhose suntan

Black briefs
Black enamel & gold shell earrings
Black lace mantilla

Act II
Opening:
  Repeat above

Grand Canal

Green I:
  Repeat black skirt, T-shirt, sandals
  Add green cape, add black hood, add green gloves, add green velvet tricorn w/mask

Green II:
  Repeat black skirt, T-shirt, sandals
  Add green velvet tricorn (no mask)

Casanova:
  Sparkle tights
  Pink teddy & corset
  Mules
  Pink mobcap w/out pink ringlets

Red Coperto:
  Repeat sparkle tights
  Add red brocade shoes, add red feather pannier
  Nude net leotard w/feather "fins" & bubbles
  White Marie Antoinette wig w/gondola trim

Finale:
  White "shawl" skirt
  White T-shirt w/bead trim
  Beige sandals
  Beige briefs

GIULIETTA

Act I
Black eyelet dress w/scattered sequin trim
Black low heel shoes
Sheer energy ntw pantyhose nude
Black opaque ntw pantyhose
Black textured "cheerios" pattern pantyhose
Bronze fish earrings
Black bangle bracelet
Black lace mantilla

Act II
Opening:
　Repeat above
Grand Canal
Green I:
　Repeat black dress, shoes
　Add: Sparkle tights, green gloves, green velvet tricorn (no mask), black turban

Green II:
　Repeat black dress, shoes, sparkle hose
　Add: Green brocade hat w/feathers

Casanova:
　Repeat sparkle tights
　Pink teddy & corset
　Pink mob cap w/pink ringlets
　Mules

Red Coperto:
　Repeat sparkle tights
　Red cape
　Red gloves
　Red hat
　Red sparkle shoes

Finale:
　White eyelet dress w/sequin trim
　White low heel shoes
　White opaque pantyhose
　White briefs

ANNABELLA

Act I
Black lace dress w/scattered sequin accents
Black "sparkle" open-toe slingbacks
Hanes alive ntw pantyhose little color
Black swiss dot pattern pantyhose
Black briefs
Black jet & crystal drop earrings
Black jet & crystal bracelet
Black lace handkerchief
Black lace mantilla

Act II
Opening:
  Repeat above
Grand Canal
Green I:
  Repeat black lace dress
  Add: Sparkle tights, green gloves, black turban, green velvet tricorn w/mask, green brocade shoes

Green II:
  Repeat dress, sparkle tights, shoes
  Add: Green brocade hat w/feathers

Casanova:
  Repeat sparkle tights
  Pink teddy & corset
  Pink mob cap w/pink ringlets
  Mules

Red Coperto:
  Repeat sparkle tights
  Red cape
  Red hat
  Red gloves
  Red sparkle shoes

Finale:
  White lace dress w/scattered sequins
  Gold & silver "net" pumps
  White opaque ntw pantyhose
  White briefs
  Crystal drop earrings
  Crystal bracelet

FRANCESCA

Act I
Black strapless dress
Black "train" w/net bustle
Black opera gloves w/bead trim
Black open-toe sling back shoes w/bead trim
Hanes alive ntw pantyhose little color
Capezio H & S ntw black pantyhose
Black briefs

Black dangle "dice" earrings
Rhinestone & black jet bracelet
Black lace mantilla

Act II
Opening:
　Repeat above
Grand Canal
Green I:
　Sparkle tights
　Green briefs
　Green pannier
　Beige net armbands w/green trim
　Green brocade shoes
　Green cape
　Green gloves
　Black hood
　Green velvet tricorn w/mask

Green II:
　Repeat sparkle tights, pannier, briefs, armbands, shoes
　Add: Green brocade hat w/feathers

Casanova I:
　Repeat sparkle tights
　Pink teddy & corset
　Pink mob cap w/pink ringlets
　White mules

Casanova II:
　Repeat tights, corset, teddy
　Add: Black "flying nuns" hat
　Red brocade shoes

Red Coperto:
　Pink sparkle briefs
　Repeat sparkle tights
　Red feather pannier w/seahorses
　Red beaded bodice w/bubble trim
　Beige net opera mitts w/bead trim
　Repeat brocade shoes

Finale:
　White strapless dress w/rhinestone trim
　White "train" w/net bustle

White open-toe sling back shoes w/bead trim
White opera gloves w/bead trim
White opaque ntw pantyhose
White briefs
2 wide rhinestone bracelets
Rhinestone earrings

DIANA

Act I
Black milliskin leotard
Black milliskin tights w/feet
Black skirt w/black patent belt
Black jacket w/jet trim
Black thigh-high boots
Black fedora w/black jet band
Black square earrings
Black lace mantilla

Act II
Opening:
  Repeat above
Grand Canal
Green I:
  Repeat leotard, skirt, jacket, boots
  Add: Sparkle tights, black hood, green velvet tricorn w/mask

Green II:
  Repeat leotard, skirt, jacket, boots, tights
  Add: Green brocade hat w/feathers

Casanova I:
  Repeat sparkle tights
  Pink teddy & corset
  Pink mob cap w/pink ringlets
  Mules

Casanova II:
  Repeat teddy, corset, sparkle tights
  Add: Black "flying nuns" hat, red brocade shoes

Red Coperto:
  Repeat sparkle tights, shoes
  Add: Pink sparkle briefs, red feather pannier, red beaded bodice w/bubbles, nude net opera mitts w/beads, white Marie Antoinette wig

Finale:
- White milliskin leotard
- White milliskin tights w/feet
- White skirt w/white patent belt
- White jacket w/rhinestone trim
- White thigh-high boots
- White fedora w/beaded band
- Rhinestone earrings

RENATA

Act I
- Black dress (velvet bodice, taffeta skirt)
- Black open-toe pumps w/ankle strap & jet trim
- Capezio H & S black ntw pantyhose
- Black briefs
- Black jet drop earrings
- Black lace mantilla

Act II
Opening:
  Repeat above
Grand Canal
Green I:
  Repeat dress
  Add: Sparkle tights, green brocade shoes, black turban, green velvet tricorn (no mask)

Green II:
  Repeat dress, shoes, sparkle tights
  Add: Green brocade hat w/feathers

Casanova:
  Repeat sparkle tights
  Pink teddy & corset
  Pink mob cap w/pink ringlets
  Mules

Red Coperto:
  Repeat sparkle tights
  Red brocade shoes
  Pink sparkle briefs
  Red feather pannier

Nude net leotard
White Marie Antoinette wig

Finale:
   White dress (velvet bodice, taffeta skirt)
   White open-toe pumps w/ankle strap
   White opaque ntw pantyhose
   White briefs
   Crystal drop earrings

OLGA VON STURM

Act I
Black dress
Black turban
Black open-toe sling back shoes
Capezio H & S ntw pantyhose suntan
Black ribbed texture ntw pantyhose
Black briefs
Gold & rhinestone drop leaf earrings
Gold & rhinestone leaf necklace
Rhinestone rings
Black lace mantilla

Act II
Opening:
   Repeat above
Grand Canal
Green I:
   Beige dress w/green sequin & bubble trim
   Beige shoes w/green trim
   Beige briefs
   Sparkle tights
   Green cape
   Green gloves
   Black hood
   Green velvet tricorn w/mask

Green II:
   Repeat dress, shoes, sparkle tights
   Add: White organdy "sheel" hat

Casanova:
   Repeat sparkle tights
   Pink teddy & corset

Pink mob cap w/pink ringlets
Mules

Red Coperto:
    Repeat sparkle tights
    Repeat beige shoes
    Red cape
    Red hat
    Red gloves

Finale:
    White dress
    White turban
    White open-toe slingback shoes
    White opaque ntw pantyhose
    White briefs
    Leaf earrings & necklace

HEIDI VON STURM

Act I
Black jumper
Black middy overblouse
Black horsehair sailor hat w/ribbons
Black patent shoes w/bows
Beige ntw pantyhose
Black opaque ntw tights
Rhinestone heart on gold chain
Gold & rhinestone heart earrings
Black lace mantilla

Act II
Opening:
    Repeat above
Grand Canal
Green I:
    Sparkle tights
    Beige briefs
    Beige dress w/green sequin & bubbles
    Beige shoes w/green trim
    Green cape
    Green gloves
    Black hood
    Green velvet tricorn w/mask

Green II:
  Repeat dress, shoes, sparkle tights
  Add: White organdy "baby bonnet"

Casanova:
  Repeat sparkle tights
  Pink teddy & corset
  Mules
  Pink mob cap w/pink ringlets

Red Coperto:
  Red cape
  Red hat
  Red gloves
  Repeat beige shoes
  Repeat sparkle tights

Finale:
  White jumper
  White middy blouse
  White horsehair sailor hat
  White shoes w/bows
  White opaque ntw pantyhose
  White briefs
  Repeat necklace
  Repeat earrings

ILSA VON AESSE

Act I
Black V-neck overblouse
Black "harem" pants
Black open-front coat
Black & gold brocade shoes
Black beaded headband
Capezio H & S ntw pantyhose suntan
Black opaque knee-hi's
Gold loops earrings w/jet drops
Black lace mantilla

Act II
Opening:
  Repeat above
Grand Canal
Green I:
  Beige overblouse w/bubble trim

    Beige "harem" pants
    Plastic coat w/green sequin & bubble trim
    Beige shoes w/green trim
    Sparkle tights
    Green cape
    Green gloves
    Black hood
    Green velvet tricorn w/mask

Green II:
    Repeat blouse, pants, coat, shoes, tights
    Add: White tulle "pouff" hat

Casanova:
    Repeat sparkle tights
    Pink teddy & corset
    Pink mob cap w/pink ringlets
    Mules

Red Coperto:
    Repeat sparkle tights
    Repeat beige shoes
    Red cape
    Red hat
    Red gloves

Finale:
    White V-neck overblouse
    White "harem" pants
    White open-front coat w/rhinestone trim
    White beaded headband
    White opaque knee-hi's
    Beige open-toe slingbacks w/gold trim
    Crystal necklace w/gold & crystal drops
    Gold loop earrings w/crystal drops

GRETCHEN VON KRUPF

Act I
Black sleeveless blouse w/net collar
Black jacket w/jet trim
Black lederhosen w/jet trimmed buttons
Black tyrol-style hat w/black feather "brush"
Black suede open-toe pumps w/bows
Sheer energy ntw pantyhose nude

Black opaque ntw pantyhose
Black textured lace pantyhose
Black & gold earrings
2 gold rings w/black stones
Black walking stick (props)
Black lace mantilla

Act II
Opening:
   Repeat above
Grand Canal
Green I:
   Sparkle tights
   Beige sleeveless blouse
   Beige jacket w/green sequin trim
   Beige lederhosen w/green sequin trim
   Beige shoes w/green trim
   Green cape
   Black hood
   Green gloves
   Green velvet tricorn w/mask

Green II:
   Repeat blouse, jacket, shorts, hose, shoes
   Add: White organdy "shell" hat

Casanova:
   Repeat sparkle tights
   Pink teddy & corset
   Pink mob cap w/pink ringlets
   Mules

Red Coperto:
   Red cape
   Red hat
   Red gloves
   Repeat beige shoes

Finale:
   White sleeveless blouse w/net collar
   White jacket w/rhinestone trim
   White lederhosen w/rhinestone buttons
   White tyrol-style hat w/feather "brush"
   White open-toe sling back shoes
   White opaque ntw pantyhose

White textured lace pantyhose
White walking stick (props)

YOUNG GUIDO'S SCHOOLMATE #1

Act I
Black dress shirt
Black sweater
Black shorts
Black ankle socks
Black sandals
Black knee pads

Act II
Grand Canal
Casanova:
  Green beaded jacket
  Green satin "knickers"
  Green milliskin tights
  Green turban w/feathers
  Green ballet slippers w/bead trim
  Black full-face mask

Finale:
  White long-sleeve dress shirt
  White sweater
  White shorts
  White ankle socks
  White sandals

YOUNG GUIDO'S SCHOOLMATE #2

Act I
Black boat-neck "stripe" shirt
Black shorts
Black socks
Black sandals
Black knee pads

Act II
Grand Canal
Casanova:
  Green beaded jacket
  Green satin "knickers"
  Green milliskin tights

Green turban w/feathers
Green ballet slippers w/bead trim
Black full-face mask

Finale:
White boat-neck "stripe" shirt
White shorts
White ankle socks
White sandals

YOUNG GUIDO'S SCHOOLMATE #3

Act I
Black T-shirt
Black shorts w/suspenders
Black ankle socks
Black sandals
Black knee pads

Act II
Grand Canal
Casanova:
Green beaded jacket
Green satin "knickers"
Green milliskin tights
Green turban w/feathers
Green ballet slippers w/bead trim
Black full-face mask

Finale:
White T-shirt
White shorts w/suspenders
White ankle socks
White sandals

ON THE TWENTIETH CENTURY
(ALL GROUPS—MUSICAL COMEDY)

Book and Lyrics by ADOLPH GREEN and BETTY COMDEN, Music by CY COLEMAN

17 principal roles, plus singers and extras (doubling possible)—Various sets

Whether performed with elaborate scenery, or on a simple skeletal scale, this brilliantly comic musical can appeal to audiences everywhere. This is truly an extravagant show—but its extravagance lies not in its scenery and physical production, but in the boisterous, tumultuous energy—and in the lush and sprightly energetic surge of its very melodic score. The story concerns the efforts of a flamboyant theatrical impressario to persuade a film star to appear in his next production, to outwit rival producers and creditors, to rid himself of religious nut Letitia Primrose (played by Imogene Coca on Broadway) and Lily's film star boyfriend Bruce Granit (who's as strong in profile as he is weak in brains). And, he must do all this before the famed 20th Century Ltd. reaches NYC! The story, and it's two leading characters—the mad impressario Oscar Jaffe and the love of his life and his greatest star Lily Garland—can be loved and enjoyed by all audiences. "Spectacular . . . funny . . . elegant . . . civilized wit and wild humor."—N.Y. Times. "A perfect musical . . . a gorgeous show!"—N.Y. Post. (#819)

KURT VONNEGUT'S GOD BLESS YOU, MR. ROSEWATER
(MUSICAL SATIRE)

By the creators of
LITTLE SHOP OF HORRORS

Book and Lyrics by HOWARD ASHMAN
Music by ALAN MENKEN
Additional lyrics by DENNIS GREEN

10 men, 4 women (principals—also double smaller roles), extras, musicians—Various interiors and exteriors

"One of Vonnegut's most affecting and likeable novels becomes an affecting and likable theatrical experience, with more inventiveness, cockeyed characters, high-muzzle-velocity dialogue and just plain energy that you get from the majority of playwrights."—Newsweek. Eliot Rosewater's a well-intentioned idealist and philanthropic nut—and as president of a multi-million family foundation dispenses money to arcane and artsy-crafty projects. He's also a World War II veteran with a guilt complex, haunted by all this wealth—and also slightly crazy. His outlandish behavior enrages his senator dad, alienates his society-conscious wife—and the money attracts a young, shyster lawyer who tries to divert it to an obscure branch of the family. It portrays Vonnegut's vision of money, avarice and human behavior—as it aims a satrical fusillade at plastic America, fast foods, trademarks, slogans, media blitzes and the follies of materialism. "A charming, delightful, unexpected and thoughtful musical."—N.Y. Post. (#630)

#W-29